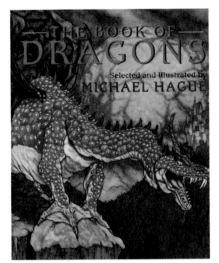

The Book of Dragons

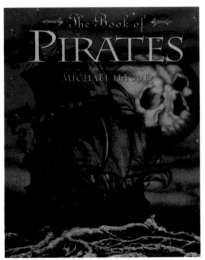

The Book of Pirates

The Book of Fairies

The Book of Fairy Poetry

The Book of
Wizards

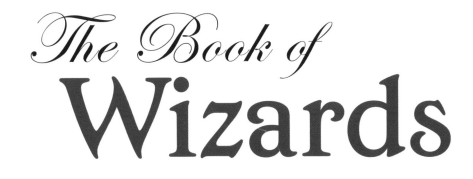

Selected and illustrated by
MICHAEL HAGUE

HarperCollinsPublishers

For Sophia and her proud parents,
Angela and Tony DiTerlizzi
—M.H.

The Book of Wizards

Copyright © 2008 by Michael Hague

Manufactured in China.

All rights reserved. No part of this book may be used or reproduced in any manner
whatsoever without written permission except in the case of brief quotations
embodied in critical articles and reviews.

For information address HarperCollins Children's Books, a division of HarperCollins
Publishers, 1350 Avenue of the Americas, New York, NY 10019.

www.harpercollinschildrens.com

Library of Congress Cataloging-in-Publication Data

The book of wizards / selected and illustrated by Michael Hague. — 1st ed.

    v.   cm.

    Contents: Baba Yaga — Coyote and the medicine woman — King Solomon's ring
— Taliessen and the magic potion — The battle of the wizards of the north — The
tempest — The black school — The enchantment of Merlin — Under Circe's spell.

    ISBN 978-0-688-14005-2 (trade bdg.)

    1. Wizards—Literary collections. [1. Wizards—Literary collections.] I. Hague,
Michael.

PZ5.B6428 2008   2007014468

813'.54080377—dc22   CIP

                                                      AC

Typography by Jeanne L. Hogle

1   2   3   4   5   6   7   8   9   10

❖

First Edition

CONTENTS

CHAPTER I

Baba Yaga

There once was a young girl named Sonya who lived in a thatch-roofed cottage on the edge of a vast forest with her father, a wood-cutter. The little girl's mother had died the previous winter and, thinking to best provide for his daughter, the woodcutter took another woman as his wife and, of course, stepmother to Sonya.

At first the three seemed happy; the stepmother looked after the house and garden while the father went each day into the forest to cut wood. In time, however, it became clear to the woman that Sonya was the apple of her husband's eye and that she would never enjoy his full affection as long as the daughter was around. How could she get rid of the girl without incurring the wrath of the father? On this question the wicked woman thought long and hard. And then the solution came to her.

One day when the father was off in the forest, the stepmother called Sonya to her and said, "I have just broken my last sewing needle and I must mend your father's shirt. Go you to the hut of Baba Yaga and fetch me a new one."

Now Sonya was an innocent young girl and had no suspicion of the evil intent that lay behind her stepmother's request. On the contrary, the girl was uncommonly generous and was only too happy that she could be of help.

"Gladly, stepmother," replied the girl. "But you must tell me the way to her house, for I don't know this Baba Yaga you speak of."

Little did Sonya dream that she was being asked to pay a call on an evil witch who was known to steal children in the night and, it was said, eat those who fell into her horrid grasp.

"Go to the third turning along the path by the forest's edge and follow it until you can go no farther, and you will come to the house of Baba Yaga," instructed the treacherous woman.

After putting on her blue kerchief, off went Sonya to do her wicked stepmother's bidding. She skipped along the path at the edge of the forest and, counting the turnings, took the third one and entered the dark woods. She had gone a few leagues along the path—farther than she had ever been from home—when she came upon a clearing where an old woman lived in a poor hut surrounded by her goats. The goatherd was at her well struggling to turn the handle that drew the pail from the bottom.

"Good day to you, old mother," said Sonya to the woman. "Let me help you with that," and she proceeded to crank the handle with her strong young arms and in a trice had a brimming pail of water sitting on the edge of the well.

"Thank you for helping an old woman," said the goatherd. "It is rare to find someone with such a generous heart. Pray tell me, what brings you to this part of the forest?"

And so Sonya told the old woman about the errand she had been sent on and how she sought the house of Baba Yaga to fetch a sewing needle for her stepmother.

At the mention of the dreaded witch's name, the old woman narrowed her eyes but gave no sign of the grave danger facing the girl. She had lived long and learned much of the way of the world, and one thing she knew was this: a good and pure heart will win out over evil. Without directly interfering—for she greatly feared the wrath of the witch—the old woman resolved to help this child as best she could.

"You have done me a good turn, so let me repay you as best I can.

As you see, I don't have much, but I can offer you the bounty of my goats, which may be of some comfort to you, as the way to Baba Yaga's hut is a long one." Accordingly, she gave Sonya a small sack containing some dried goat meat, some cheese, and a little bit of butter wrapped in a twist of paper.

Off went the unsuspecting girl, deeper and deeper into the forest. As the sun went down, the path became difficult to see in the half-light of dusk, and it seemed that branches reached out to pluck at her clothes and hair. Before, the path was smooth, but now rocks and roots seemed to rise up to trip her feet. Just before the sun went down, Sonya came around a bend in the trail and saw a remarkable sight.

By the side of the path, behind a white picket fence, was a small cottage that stood on what appeared to be two columns. Drawing nearer, Sonya could see that the columns were actually two gigantic chicken legs that were currently turning the whole house slowly in circles! Getting closer, she could also see that the picket fence was actually made of human leg and arm bones! A pack of hungry-looking dogs milled around the house and set up a din of snarling and barking.

Sonya was very frightened now and didn't know whether to go back in the darkness or stay and complete her task. Suddenly the house stopped turning and she could see a door that appeared to be the mouth of the house and, above it, two windows on either side

that looked just like eyes.

"Welcome to the house of Baba Yaga," said the door as it opened, its rusty hinges shrieking loudly. "Come, I'll kneel down so that you can enter." And with that the house squatted down on its giant hen's legs so that the girl could reach the doorsill. Quaking with fright, the girl had no choice but to do as she was bidden and so stepped up and into the cottage.

Though it appeared to be small from the outside, once Sonya was in it, the house seemed much larger. A fire was burning in a grate in what appeared to be the kitchen, with a jet black cat lazily curled up in front of it. When it saw the girl, the cat rose and, stretching, arched its back and said, "What brings you to the house of Baba Yaga, little girl?"

Having gotten over her surprise at a talking door, Sonya found the idea of a cat speaking to her even less surprising, and she told the animal about the errand her stepmother had sent her on.

"My mistress is gone tonight but will return in the morning. If you wish, you may lie here by the fire and sleep alongside of me," said the cat, indicating a place by the hearth.

Sonya was grateful for the kind offer and, sitting down next to the cat, said, "You look hungry and I have this piece of cheese. I would be pleased to share it with you." The cat was indeed very hungry and accepted the girl's offer. After the two had eaten, Sonya, very tired from her journey, wrapped herself in her cloak and was soon fast

asleep in front of the glowing fire.

She slept soundly until morning, when the sound of the rusty hinges of the door woke the girl with a start and she looked up to see the horrible figure Baba Yaga, who had just returned from her night's travels. Sonya had never seen anyone quite like the crone in front of her. A mere five feet tall and appearing shorter due to a hunched back, Baba Yaga had a narrow, pinched face that peered out of a scraggly mop of thinning white hair. Her skin was sallow, and her long nose nearly curved down to meet her bony pointed chin. When she opened her mouth, Sonya could see her dreadful jagged teeth made of iron. The witch was clad in a dress of grayish-brown homespun cloth that had faded with time and was covered with patches where the fabric had torn and been crudely mended.

"What is it you want, my pretty young thing?" said the sorceress as she hungrily eyed the girl. "Is there something you seek from Baba Yaga?"

"I—I—I have been sent by my step-m-mother to fetch a new sewing needle with which to m-mend my father's shirt," the terrified young girl managed to stutter.

"Oh ho!" replied the witch, who knew a thing or two about step-mothers. "Of course I will give you a needle. But first you must refresh yourself from your long journey. My servant girl will fill a bath for you so that you may wash yourself. I will leave you now but will return in one hour." With that the sorceress went into her chamber in another part of the house, where she began to prepare an herbal decoction that would make the girl taste even sweeter.

Sonya was then led to a room at the rear of the house where a bathtub was suspended over a fire, though to call it a bathtub would not be entirely accurate, for it was more in the nature of a kettle, and it was the intent of the witch to boil the girl and eat her for dinner that day.

The servant girl began to help Sonya undress before her "bath,"

and though Sonya's clothes were plain, compared to the other girl's rags they seemed regal. Sonya noticed the girl's envious gaze, so she said, "Would you like my kerchief? It would look very nice with those blue eyes of yours. Mine are brown, so they really don't match."

The girl was so grateful at this kindly gesture that she broke out in tears and confided in Sonya. The servant girl told her that Baba Yaga planned to boil and eat her and that she should make her getaway immediately. She also gave Sonya a magical green comb and a piece of blue ribbon and instructed her as to how they should be used.

An hour later, Baba Yaga returned and found the tub empty and no fire burning beneath it. She shrieked at the servant girl, "What has become of the little girl I asked you to prepare for my dinner?"

The girl replied, "You never gave me so much as a rag, but she gave me her beautiful blue kerchief. Maybe I looked the other way and she escaped."

"Escaped!" cried the witch. "No one escapes from my enchanted house!" And with that she rushed into the other room, where she found the black cat cleaning his whiskers by the fire.

"Where is the girl?" said the sorceress. "Why did you not scratch out her eyes to stop her from leaving?"

"Because she gave me tasty goat cheese to eat for my supper. You give me nothing and tell me to catch wretched mice," replied the cat.

Rushing to the door of the house, Baba Yaga demanded, "Why didn't I hear your hinges creak when the girl went out through you?"

The door replied, "Because she spread soothing butter on my hinges so they don't pain me anymore. You never spared me even one drop of oil."

With this the furious witch climbed into a large mortar, and pushing it with a long pestle made from a human bone, she clattered out the door and onto the pathway in front of the house. As she was leaving the yard, she hissed at the pack of dogs, "What good are you lazy curs. How is it the girl got past you without so much as a whimper or bark from any of you?"

"The nice girl gave us some delicious goat meat," replied the leader of the pack of dogs. "You haven't fed us so much as a dry bone."

Baba Yaga was in a blind, raging fury. She gnashed her teeth, which sent sparks flying in the wind as she violently beat the ground with her pestle, propelling the mortar at a terrific rate over the ground after the fleeing girl. Meanwhile, Sonya was not far ahead, though hurrying with all the speed she could manage. Every once in a while she stopped and put her ear to the ground, listening for the sound of the witch's mortar as it clattered through the forest. It wasn't too long before Baba Yaga was nearly upon the girl. Remembering the servant girl's instructions, Sonya threw the blue ribbon behind her, which, when it hit the forest floor, turned into a raging river.

"Curse that brat!" cried the sorceress, who had to take the time to round up a great herd of cattle to drink the enchanted river dry before she could resume her chase.

Sonya continued as before, running as fast as she could but stopping now and then to listen for the approach of the witch. Once again she heard the scrape of the mortar getting nearer. This time she threw the green comb into the air behind her. When it fell to earth, out of its tines sprang a thick hedgerow of spiky thorns. When she saw this, Baba Yaga attacked the dense shrubbery, chewing furiously at it with her fearsome iron teeth. But the enchanted hedge was too much for her, so eventually she gave up and, with a last curse flung in the direction of the fleeing girl, Baba Yaga slunk back to her house on the giant chicken legs.

Sonya didn't stop again until she was home at the cottage by the edge of the forest. Her father was home and extremely worried, for the girl had been gone a day and a night and most of a day.

"My darling daughter," cried the man. "Where have you been all this time?"

Catching her breath, the exhausted girl wept with relief. In between sobs she told him how the stepmother had told her to visit the house of Baba Yaga and of the terrible events that took place there. Finally she related the story of her escape and the help she had received from the strange inhabitants of the house on the giant hen's legs. Upon hearing this account, the woodcutter flew into a black

rage, thundering in a mighty voice the terrible things he would do to his wife when he found her.

The stepmother, meanwhile, had been in the garden and had seen Sonya's return and heard her tearful reunion with her father. Seeing the murderous rage that had consumed her husband and knowing what would befall her if she fell into his hands, she quickly fled into the forest, never to be seen or heard from again.

And Sonya lived happily in the cottage by the edge of the forest with her father—who never married again—and people would come by to visit and hear the incredible story of how the girl with the generous heart escaped from the clutches of Baba Yaga.

CHAPTER II

Coyote and the Medicine Woman

Long ago, when buffalo roamed the plains in numbers too great to count, there lived a wise Indian woman. She lived alone in a large white buffalo-hide tepee by a lake. Though she neither fished nor hunted, there was always food for her cook pot. No one knew how she came by her provisions, but it was rumored that she was skilled in the magical arts and thus was provided for. And this was true; taught by her mother who in turn was taught by her mother, the young woman was the last of a line of powerful medicine women.

One day as she was eating some buffalo stew by a fire in front of her tepee, Coyote came trotting by. He sniffed the air hungrily.

"My, that smells good," said the wily wolf-dog. "Would you have some to spare for a hungry fellow like me?"

"If you are willing to work for your dinner," replied the medicine woman.

So it was agreed that in return for his supper Coyote would fetch wood for the woman's fire and scrape the eating vessels clean with sand by the lakeside when they were done eating. And one meal led

to another and then another. The days passed, and since both were content with the arrangement, they lived peaceably together in the large white buffalo-hide tepee by the lake.

It came to pass that one day there was no more meat to cook. Noticing this, the medicine woman said to Coyote, "I have a desire for some of those purple berries that grow in the marsh on the other side of the lake. Please fetch me some."

"That I will," said Coyote, trotting off with a rush basket with which to gather the fruit.

When he was gone and out of sight, the medicine woman ducked under the flap that served as the door to the tepee and entered. Reaching high up to a hook on one of the tent poles, she took down a big black buffalo horn. Returning to the fire outside, the woman threw a handful of sweet grass onto the blaze, and a cloud of white smoke rose into the air. Holding the horn in the smoke, the medicine woman uttered the sacred words she had been taught, and in an instant seven tall, strongly muscled braves appeared. These were her spirit-brothers who provided her with the food she needed.

Without a word, the seven braves went off in search of meat for the woman's cook pot. Magically, within minutes they returned laden with a skinned and butchered buffalo and gave it to the woman. She smiled her thanks and, as she uttered another incantation, the seven spirit-brothers turned to smoke and disappeared back into the buffalo horn.

When Coyote returned a little while later, his keen nose soon detected the great cache of meat near the tepee. But saying nothing, as was his nature, he merely gave the woman the basket of purple berries that he had gathered.

The medicine woman and Coyote went about their business for another week and the supply of meat dwindled. Seeing that there remained only a single buffalo steak, the woman said to Coyote, "I have a craving for some watercress. Please go to the stream that flows into the lake and gather some for me."

Again Coyote did the bidding of the woman, and when he returned there was another store of meat near the tepee. Another week passed, and the woman sent Coyote to seek the eggs of the sage grouse that nested on the prairie a little ways off. But this time the suspicious Coyote pretended to trot off on his errand but, when he was out of sight of the camp, circled back and hid behind a blackberry bush not far from the tepee.

Once again, as Coyote watched from his hiding place, the medicine woman passed the magical buffalo horn through the smoke of the sweet grass and her seven spirit-brothers appeared to do her bidding.

Hmmm, thought Coyote to himself. If I owned such a horn, I would never be hungry again.

Returning later to the tepee with a clutch of eggs in a basket, Coyote said nothing to the woman but resolved to bide his time

until he had a chance to steal the buffalo horn. A few days later he saw his chance: the medicine woman was paying a visit to a tribal elder who was ailing and required her healing powers. Waiting until she was out of sight, Coyote went into the tepee, leaped up, and took the buffalo horn from its hook on the tent pole.

Coyote took the horn and some sweet grass and ran to a secluded clearing in the woods not far from the camp. Lighting a small fire, he threw some of the sweet grass into it and saw the white smoke begin to rise up into the air. Coyote then held the enchanted buffalo horn in the smoke as he had seen the medicine woman do. But he didn't know the sacred words needed to summon the spirit-hunters. When nothing happened, Coyote became angry and shouted at the horn, "Where are your mighty warriors? Why don't they appear for me?"

Suddenly Coyote felt something shaking within the buffalo horn.

"Ah, now I'll have those seven hunters to do my bidding," said the wolf-dog.

A loud buzzing sound was coming from the horn. Then, as Coyote stared with growing apprehension, a huge swarm of bees emerged from the horn and began to bite the hapless animal. Yelping and snapping his jaws at the stinging insects, Coyote ran as fast as he could to the lake, where he plunged into the water and lay there submerged with only his nose sticking out so he could breathe. The swarm of bees eventually disappeared, leaving a wet, sore, and very abashed Coyote to slink back to the tepee.

The medicine woman had returned—as had, magically, the buffalo horn—and she was now squatting in front of the fire, stirring her cook pot.

With a knowing glance at the bedraggled wolf-dog, she said, "Anything of interest happen while I was gone?"

"Nothing to speak of," growled Coyote. And they didn't. The medicine woman went about her work and Coyote did his chores and they lived a contented life. And Coyote would ever faithfully trot off to do any errand the woman might send him on, and he never touched the enchanted buffalo horn again.

CHAPTER III

King Solomon's Ring

Long, long ago, before your grandfather's grandfather was born, there lived in the far north a terrible creature that was feared by man and beast alike. No one knew where it had come from—some say from the depths of hell itself—but it was making its way southward and terrorizing one kingdom, then another until people feared that the whole world would fall prey to this marauding monster.

The dragon had a body like that of a giant lion, with powerful hind legs like those of a kangaroo, with which it could leap great distances over lakes or rivers or anything else in its way. Its forelegs were short, with cruel daggerlike claws that could slice a man in half in a trice. Its head resembled a crocodile's, with a long snout and jaws lined with rows of serrated teeth that, should it lose one, would immediately be replaced by another.

Nothing could hurt the beast, for it was covered in scales that were harder than steel. It had a long prehensile tail that would lash out like a whip, grasping the unwary in its coils, much like a boa constrictor. It never slept, and its two huge eyes seemed to burn from within, hypnotizing anyone foolish enough to look into them.

The beast would sit at a crossroads or the entrance to a village, devouring any unfortunate creature that came within reach, moving to another location when it had depleted that part of the country-side. The neighboring kings all offered great riches to anyone who could destroy the monster, but though many tried, none succeeded. Men tried catapults that hurled huge stones, but they just bounced off the scaly armor. Others poured great cauldrons of boiling oil on the monster, who just shook the burning liquid off like a dog would water. The beast had once been seen lying in a dense stand of pines, but when men had burned the forest down in an attempt to kill it, the creature seemed only to grow stronger in the blazing inferno.

It was widely believed that the only person who could defeat this monster was one who wielded the power of King Solomon's ring. Unfortunately no one knew where to find the ring and, if found, how to decipher the inscription within it to unlock the awesome power of the ring. One day a young lad with a stout heart and a taste for adventure came before his king and made this bold statement: "Sire, I wish to go in search of the ring that will enable me to slay the dragon that threatens your kingdom. If I succeed, I will ask you for the hand of your daughter in marriage."

Now the king had seen many men try and fail to defeat the dragon, and he didn't think this lad would have any better luck, but he also had no other alternative, so he replied, "Go then and seek the ring of power, and if you can kill the beast then I will gladly make you my son and heir."

And so the lad set out, traveling east for many weeks, crossing countless rivers and climbing over three great mountain chains until he came to the wisest man in that land where wisdom is prized above all virtues. He explained his quest to the magus (which is another name for a sorcerer who practices white magic) and asked his advice on how to find King Solomon's ring.

"It is well that you have come to me, lad," said the wise old man, "for though it has long been lost to me, I know its secrets, and if you bring it to me I will show you how to release its power."

"But where can I find it?" asked the boy.

"In truth, I cannot tell you," replied the magus, "but if you stay and do my bidding for one year, I will teach you the language of the birds and they can be your guide, for birds fly everywhere and see many things that are hidden from men."

So the boy stayed with the wise man and helped him by fetching wood and water for the old man's cottage. He also learned to gather the plants and roots needed to make healing medicines and potions that the man used to cure the people that came to him from far and wide. In return for these chores, every day the man taught the boy a little bit more about the language of birds. As with any language, first he learned how to make simple sounds, then simple words until, finally, as the year was nearly ended, he found that he could actually

understand what birds say to each other.

What a wonder! Understanding the language of birds opened up a whole new world to the boy. Most of what he heard concerned the daily needs of birds: one told another where to find a cherry tree that had just ripened; another revealed where a farmer was ploughing a field, exposing juicy fat worms for the taking. Occasionally the boy heard other things about the goings on in the village (for birds love to talk about the follies of mankind). In this way the lad picked up details—some quite scandalous—about the people in the surrounding countryside, and it helped to pass the long days of his servitude.

Finally the year came to an end and the young man filled his knapsack with some morsels of food, bid good-bye to the wise old sorcerer, and set off in search of King Solomon's ring. As he walked day after day, he never felt lonely, for he had all the birds of the air as company. The lad learned many things: why the rooster crows (because he's mischievous and likes to wake people) and why the magpie steals shiny objects (because they look pretty in his nest). But the weeks went by, and he heard nothing about the ring that he sought.

Then a wonderful thing happened, and this is how it came about. One morning as the young man was eating his morning bread by the side of a stream, a sparrow flew down from a tree and hopped up to him, tilting his little head this way and that.

"Will you spare a crumb for a hungry friend?" said the sparrow.

"That I will, and gladly," said the boy.

"Much obliged," said the bird, who seemed not at all surprised that the lad spoke the language of the birds—he had come to know that men were capable of many strange things.

"You look to be on a journey," said the bird. "What is it you seek?"

So the young man told the sparrow about the monster of the north and how he sought King Solomon's ring to help him slay the beast. After a while—and a few more crumbs—the sparrow flitted away through the trees and perched on a branch above a big black crow, to which he confided the purpose of the boy's quest. Then the crow flapped out of the tree down to a cornfield where a dozen of his fellow crows were feeding. In between beakfuls of corn kernels, the crow related what the sparrow had told him earlier. And so from sparrow to crow to nightingale to titmouse to cardinal went the question: "Do you know where to find King Solomon's ring?"

A few days later the cardinal happened to be speaking with a wise old fish hawk and related the tale of the boy's quest. Said the bird, "The ring the boy seeks is possessed by a sorceress who disguises herself as a beautiful maiden. She lives nowhere and everywhere through the magic of the ring."

"Then how can the boy ever find her and the ring?" asked the cardinal.

"There is a lake where I sometimes hunt, and the sorceress, in the form of a fair maiden, comes to it to wash her face by the light of the full moon. It is said to be a magical lake whose water preserves the witch's beauty and youth," replied the fish hawk.

And so, knowing where the lake could be found, the cardinal told the titmouse who, in turn, told the nightingale who told the crow who told the sparrow who told the young man who was, as you can imagine, extremely pleased that he finally knew the whereabouts of King Solomon's ring. He resolved to set out that very day to find the magical lake, following the fish hawk's directions.

It took the lad a week of steady walking, first through a valley, then over a hill to another. He trekked through a moor dotted with craggy tors and then through a boggy swamp, where he stepped up to his waist in fetid mud before he finally wrested himself free and reached drier ground. On the seventh day he found the lake the fish hawk had directed him to and he set about looking for a place to hide and await the coming of the witch-maiden. He circled the small lake and noticed a large weeping willow tree located on one side at the water's edge. He hoisted himself up into the tree and nestled comfortably in a crotch—hidden by the long hanging branches of the willow—and waited. . . .

He must have dozed off, being very tired from his travels, and when he awoke it was dark, and through the canopy of the willow's leaves he could faintly see the full moon rising over the lake. After a while, the boy heard a faint rustling sound and saw a shimmering outline of a young woman approach the lake not far from where he hid. He saw her kneel down and, while softly murmuring an incantation, bathe her face three times. Straining to hear her words, the young man thought he heard her sing:

"In the light of Luna bright
By this sacred lake tonight
I ask you, goddess, in a song
To keep me fair and keep me young."

The lad had never heard such a beguiling voice and longed to see the face of the girl who sang so sweetly. But when he parted the willow branches, the maiden saw the motion and cried out, "Who is it who spies on me in the night?!! Show yourself or you will suffer the consequences."

Now the young man knew the awful power of the ring and knew he must do as he was bidden. So, lowering himself to the ground, he bowed before the maiden and said, "Forgive me, kind mistress. I am just a poor traveler who, like a wandering bird, took refuge in this tree to ward off the evils of the night. And I only looked out to see who it was who sang so sweetly. I see now that the face that sang far surpasses the song for beauty."

These words greatly pleased the maiden, who also liked the rugged good looks of the young man before her. "Very well, my young swain. Why don't you leave your roost and stay with me in my castle. I assure you a feather bed will be softer and warmer than that nest of wood that you've been used to."

So the youth went with the maiden to a beautiful castle that seemed to shimmer with glints of gold and silver in the moonlight. Entering the great entrance hall, the boy was struck with wonder at the sumptuous furnishings: beautiful tapestries covering the walls, soft woven carpets underfoot, giant silver candelabras and crystal chandeliers lit with thousands of clear-burning candles. The maiden led the boy to the dining room, where a sumptuous feast had been laid out on a long linen-covered table. After they had eaten and drunk to a sufficiency, the maiden said, "You must be tired from your journey. I will take you to your chamber now." And with that he was shown into a bedroom as big as a cottage with a bed that could have slept ten. With words of gratitude he sank into the soft

down mattress and was soon in a deep, dreamless sleep.

The next morning the young man awoke to see the sun shining brightly and, opening the large window, saw below him a splendid garden with flowers of every kind all abloom. Beyond, he could see an orchard with all manner of trees: apple, pear, quince, plum, orange, and lemon—all in fruit. This is very strange, thought the boy. It was early winter in the country I traveled in yesterday, and yet here it's spring, summer, and autumn all at once.

While he was pondering this conundrum, a small bird alighted on the windowsill. "Good morning," said the chickadee.

"Good day to you," said the lad.

"I've heard from my friend the cardinal that you seek the ring of King Solomon. You are under the roof of the current owner, though things are not as they seem, as you will see. Whatever you do, don't give the sorceress your blood. If you do, you will forfeit your soul. Remember, not a drop!" And with that, the bird flew off.

The sorceress-maiden came to the boy later that morning, and she appeared even more beautiful than the night before. "Let me show you around my castle," she said, and she proceeded to show him one room after another filled with all manner of precious objects. In fact, there was nothing there at all. The castle and all its rooms and furnishings, all the treasures, like the maiden's appearance, were all produced by enchantment through the power of King Solomon's ring. Without its power all would be swept away like the wind.

"As you can see," she said when they had returned and sat in the garden sipping refreshing fruit sherbets, "I have pearls, diamonds, and rubies, gold and silver beyond measure, with servants to obey my every whim. All I lack is someone to share all this with. I am lonely and I have come to like you and ask you now if you will marry me and be king of all this. Like me, you will never grow old and gray; you will always appear as you do now—a handsome, strong young man in the prime of youth."

The lad's head was spinning with all that he had seen and heard that day, but he remembered the warning the bird had given him and he was wary.

"Let me think about this magnificent offer, fair maiden. I am still weary from the road and scarcely trust my eyes and ears not to deceive me. Let me stay awhile and think this over."

"Very well, my sleeper-in-trees," said the maiden. "I will wait until the next full moon for an answer. Till then I will show you the exquisite pleasures that can be yours for all eternity."

And so the days and weeks flew by, and the maiden made good on her promise to show the young man joys and pastimes that he could partake of with her in her enchanted world. One day the maiden took the lad to a secret chamber that he had not seen before. On a gold table was an ornate silver casket. Pulling a small gold key from around her neck and opening the box, the maiden said, "Here is my greatest treasure of all: a ring that was wrought in ancient times by the wisest king to ever live. The power of the one who wears it is unmatched by anyone on earth."

The sorceress-maiden went on to explain the powers given to one who wears the ring. "If I put it on the middle finger of my left hand, I can fly like the swiftest bird. If I wear it on the little finger, I become invisible. If it is on the middle finger of my right hand, no harm can befall me. When I wear it on my right forefinger, I can create anything I wish just by thinking it. And when it is on my right thumb, that arm is as strong as a score of men. This, too, I will share with you if you agree to be my husband. All that I ask in return is a token of your devotion: give me a drop of blood from the palm of your right hand to be mingled with mine."

The youth was agog at being so close to that which he had sought for so long. But when he heard the maiden's request and recalled the bird's warning—"Don't give her your blood . . . not a drop!"—he suppressed a shudder from the fear that ran down his spine. This will take some clever thinking if I am to gain the ring and not lose my soul to this enchantress, the youth thought to himself. Then, feigning an air of indifference, he said to the maiden, "I have heard tales of such things around the fire as a boy, but forgive me if I say I can scarcely believe that this ring can do all that you claim."

"Let me prove it to you then," said the maiden, and, so saying, she put the ring on the middle finger of her right hand.

"Now take that dagger and stab me," she said to the lad. He was

unwilling at first, but she pressed him, and so, gently at first, then with real force, he pressed the sharp blade into the maiden's arm. It didn't even make a dent in the skin. It was as if an invisible shield had come between the knife and the arm. Then the maiden put the ring on the little finger of her left hand and she vanished before the youth's eyes. A few seconds later she appeared again, holding the ring in the palm of her hand and laughing.

Sensing her good mood, the lad said, "Let me see for myself if the ring will work these magical tricks with me." Wanting to sway the youth to grant her wish to be married and suspecting no treachery from the innocent-looking lad, she complied by slipping the ring on the middle finger of his right hand. She took the dagger and jabbed at the lad's arm as he had done to her. There was nary a mark to be seen. The youth even tried to cut himself, to no avail. Then the young man asked her to show him the great strength the ring could give to the wearer. Complying, she led him outside to the orchard and put the ring on his right thumb.

"Move that apple tree," the maiden commanded. To his astonishment, the lad was able to pull the apple tree out of the ground as if it had been no more than a carrot. Laughing with the pleasure such power brought him and suddenly realizing that the time was at hand to obtain the object of his long quest, the young man slipped the ring onto the little finger of his left hand and, of course, vanished from sight.

Still in the giddy mood created by the feats the ring had displayed, laughingly the maiden said, "See, the ring works for you as well as I. Now come, let me see that handsome face that will be mine to enjoy forever when we wed."

But the young man had what he wanted, and without a sound he crept between the fruit trees of the orchard until he reached a meadow on the other side. He thought for a moment, trying to recall the maiden's instructions. Then he deftly switched the ring onto the middle finger of his left hand, whereupon he reappeared and shot up into the air like a flushed grouse and swiftly flew away to the west.

Had the youth looked back, he would have seen an astonishing sight: where the orchard and garden had been, there was a swampy marsh. Instead of the beautiful castle, there was a tumbledown, one-room hut with half its thatched roof missing and the rest covered in moss. And there was no fair maiden to be seen. Only a bent-backed, ancient crone who stood in front of the hovel shaking a bony fist at the receding figure of the flying youth, with tears of rage coursing down her sunken, wrinkled face.

The lad flew until, at last, he came to the cottage of the wise old man who had taught him the language of birds. The magus was overjoyed to see again the lad who had spent a year as his apprentice. He was also thrilled to learn that the young man had procured King Solomon's ring.

"If you will bide as my guest for one month, in that time I will be able to learn many wondrous things from this ring," said the magus. "And at the end of that month, I will tell you what you need to destroy that terrible dragon of the north."

Eager to please the one who had been so helpful in his quest, the young man took his leisure, catching up on the gossip of the village—from his friends the birds—while the wise man spent many hours each day poring over the runes that were inscribed within and without the magical ring.

At the end of the month, the old sorcerer said to the young man, "I have learned more than I could have hoped from secrets locked within this ring. And though it has been used for evil in the past, as you well know, there is much it can achieve for good as well." So saying, the sorcerer instructed the youth as to how to slay the creature that threatened to ruin his homeland. The lad listened attentively to the instructions, asking questions as they arose, and finally felt confident that he could do what legions of brave men before him could not.

As he was taking his leave of the wise man, the boy said, "I am

greatly in your debt, worthy magus. When I have completed my task, I shall return and give you anything your heart should desire."

"Thank you my boy," said the good sorcerer. "But nothing you could offer me could be a greater reward than the wisdom I have gained through the study of this great ring of Solomon that you have recovered from its evil exile. Go now and complete your task as we have planned and enjoy the fruits of your long and arduous quest."

With that the young man once again slipped the ring on his finger and flew off with the speed of a falcon. He flew like the wind for three days and three nights, over three great mountain chains and countless rivers, until he reached the kingdom far to the north where his ordeal awaited him.

When he arrived in his native land, the youth set about making preparations as the wise sorcerer had instructed him. First, with the ring on his right forefinger, he fashioned a lifelike statue of a large stallion standing with its mouth wide open, its four legs deeply embedded in the rock beneath. Though cunningly realistic on the outside, inside the statue was constructed of the strongest iron. The cavity of the statue was hollow with a trapdoor hidden beneath. Next he fashioned a stout spear—exactly five feet in length—with sharp blades on both its ends. This he hid in the body of the horse statue after first attaching a sturdy length of chain to the shaft of the spear. When all was ready, the young man slipped the ring onto the middle finger of his left hand, and he

sprang into the air to go in search of the monster.

He flew high up so that he could survey the surrounding country-side for miles around. And as he rose, he saw an eagle not far away, effortlessly soaring in lazy circles on a thermal updraft of air.

"Hello, my friend," said the youth. "Will you help me find the dragon from the north that has plagued both man and beast these past three years? You fly so high and have the sharpest eyes of all. Have you seen the monster?"

"I have and will gladly take you to the place I saw him last," replied the noble bird. So saying, with the barest tilt of a wing, the eagle soared off with the lad following in its wake. They flew for the better part of twenty leagues and then, with a dip of its wing, the eagle said, "There is the monster you seek, lying at the crossroads below."

Thanking the bird for its service, the boy plunged down, down, to face the dreaded beast at last. It was time to put into action the plan that the old sorcerer had taught him.

The dragon had taken up a position behind a haystack near one corner of the crossroads so that unwary travelers would come within reach of that awful tail and so become its next meal. The youth, staying well out of range of its grasp, alighted and shouted at the dragon, "Why do you waste your time eating the scrawny peasants who live around here? You can do better than that. I can take you to a fat, meaty horse that would equal ten of the underfed scraps that you've been eating." The lad spoke in bird-speak because it is a distant relative to the language of dragons.

"Lead on," said the dragon in a deep, rumbling voice (for there is nothing dragons love more than horseflesh). "But this stallion had better be what you claim, or *you* will be my next meal, little 'man-who-flies'."

With that, the dragon made a mighty leap with its huge hind legs in the lad's direction. Anticipating this, the youth was already in the air and flew in the direction of where he had laid his trap, alighting to allow the dragon to catch up, then flying off again. In this manner, the long leaps of the monster quickly covered the distance to where the horse statue stood. On his last flight of the journey, the young man deliberately flew just beyond the horse and, upon alighting, quickly switched the ring to the little finger of his left hand. Thus cloaked in invisibility, he ran to the statue and slipped up into the belly of the "horse," shutting the trapdoor behind him.

Peering out the open mouth of the statue, the youth saw the dragon, having made its last leap, slowly approach the sturdy figure of the horse. When the monster was still a score of paces away, in the blink of an eye the serpentine tail of the beast whipped forward to grasp the horse. Though the dragon heaved mightily, the statue didn't budge an inch, so securely was it embedded in the rock beneath.

"Hmmm," rumbled the monster. "You're an uncommonly stout horse to resist my tail's power. Let us see how you resist my teeth." And with that, the dragon leaped at the horse, jaws agape, revealing the rows of flesh-tearing teeth. Meanwhile, within the statue, the young man was prepared for the attack. As the dragon's jaws closed around the head of the horse, the lad rammed the double-ended spear through the open mouth of the statue, impaling one end in the lower jaw of the dragon and, thrusting upward, driving the other blade into the roof of the dragon's terrible mouth. An ear-shattering roar shook the lad where he lay hidden. The monster recoiled from the searing pain but could only retreat the length of the strong chain that tethered the spear to the statue. The spear, made to exactly fit the beast's maw, held fast, as did the chain, and the dragon was held captive. The lad, still invisible, quietly lowered himself from the statue and made his escape.

After three days the dragon was so weakened by hunger and loss of blood that it could not even stand. So, with King Solomon's ring on his right thumb, the young man approached the beast, and with one mighty blow of a club that ten men could not lift, he ended the long reign of terror of the dragon of the north.

When word spread that the monster had been slain, there was great joy in the hearts of men, from the lowliest peasant to the greatest of lords. Church bells rang and there was dancing in the street and the lad was carried on the shoulders of the people to the throne room of the king.

"You have done as you promised," said the king to the youth, "and now I will keep my part of the bargain." And with that he summoned his daughter (who, it seemed to the lad, had only grown in beauty while he had been away) and blessed their union as man and wife. And they lived and prospered, had many children, and, in time, ruled as king and queen of the kingdom. But the young man never told a soul about the ring. So great was its power that he feared the consequences of revealing its existence. In times of trouble he might use it to defend the kingdom against enemies, but no one, not even his beloved queen, ever knew about the existence of King Solomon's ring.

As the king lay dying many years later, a curious thing happened: a magpie that the king kept as a pet was seen leaving the king's bedroom window with a glint of silver in its beak. Before anyone could catch it, it flapped away to the east and was never seen again.

seeking revenge on him for his carelessness.

With scarcely a thought, the boy instantly took the shape of a hare and, bounding on powerful hind legs, began to run. But Bronwyn was close behind and changed herself into a greyhound and streaked after him in pursuit.

"You won't escape from me, thief!" cried the witch.

Seeing this, the lad dove into the sea and turned himself into a seal and swam as fast as he could. The witch turned herself into a killer whale and sped after her prey, snapping at his sleek form with her wide jaws and terrible sharp teeth. With a great burst of speed, Daffyd propelled himself out of the water and into the air, where he transformed himself into a dove that flew off into a cloud bank. Bronwyn followed the boy and, with a mighty leap, emerged from the sea and turned into a hawk. With the raptor's keen eyesight, the sorceress soon spied the dove and swooped down on the smaller bird.

Now over land, the boy looked down on a farmyard where a farmer had recently threshed some wheat. Plunging down, Daffyd landed amid the winnowed wheat and became a grain himself. Seeing this, the sorceress changed into an enormous black hen and promptly scratched up and swallowed the seed that the boy had become.

After a little time had passed, the great bird squatted and laid a huge egg, which hatched, revealing Daffyd in his natural form as a boy. Changing into her own natural state, Bronwyn seized the lad and bound him tightly with the cord that the wheat sheaves had been

tied with. Since the potion had made him nearly as powerful as herself, the sorceress could not kill him outright. Instead, she put the unconscious lad into a leather sack and threw it into the millrace that ran past the farm.

"There, you traitorous brat! Let the river decide your fate," spat the sorceress.

Down the stream floated the sack with the boy within, whirling and eddying with the current. Mile after mile the stream flowed, bearing its captive passenger until suddenly it came to stop: the leather bag had become entangled in a fish trap that had been set in the river. The weir was owned by King Ranof and was tended by his ne'er-do-well son, Gavin, who lived with his wife in a little cottage by the side of the river. When Gavin went to check the trap in the morning, instead of the fish he was hoping for, he found the sodden leathern sack.

"What have we here?" said the man. "A queer-looking catch indeed."

Gavin pulled the sack out of the water and, slinging it over his shoulder, carried it to his cottage, where his wife awaited.

"Where are the fish we were to sell at the market?" she asked in a peevish voice. "Your luck has gone from bad to worse," she added.

"You are always so pessimistic, wife," replied Gavin. "Who knows but that this bag may contain the key to our future."

And so saying, he cut the cord that the witch had sealed the sack with and drew forth the boy within.

At the sight of the boy's face, Gavin exclaimed, "What a handsome face! I shall call him Taliessen, and we shall raise him as our son."

And so the poor couple, who were childless, raised the boy, who soon grew into a fine young man. And it appeared that their luck had changed, too. It seemed like anything that Taliessen was given to do became a success. When put in charge of the fish traps, he skillfully arranged them so that the river always filled them with fish. And when he was sent to the market, he would sell his goods at a much better price than anyone else got. When he bought provisions, he bargained skillfully and always had some extra coins to return to his grateful parents.

When the boy was sixteen, his adoptive father told him it was time for him to meet his grandfather, King Ranof. Now it should be said that the king had a very low opinion of his youngest son, Gavin, and, apart from the use of the fish weir, gave him nothing to ease his poverty. Nonetheless, the poor fisherman felt that Taliessen should meet his king and instructed him as to how to reach the castle.

Off Taliessen went to find the castle of his father's father. On the way he saw many things that were new to him, yet familiar too, through the magic of the three drops of the sorceress's potion. He could name all the plants in the fields that he passed and every sort of tree in the forest. He knew where the red fox lived and what and where it hunted. He knew where the long-necked geese had come

from and where they were flying to. Suffice it to say, the journey passed quickly and he was never bored with so much to think about and discover.

At last the lad arrived at King Ranof's castle. After being kept waiting for some time in a drafty antechamber, Taliessen was finally admitted to the throne room of the king. Asked to identify himself, the boy said:

> *"I am a shape changer of land and sea and air.*
> *I have been fish, fowl, and runner in the brake;*
> *I was then a seed and thrice born was I.*
> *Daffyd I was born in the misty isles of Cymru*
> *But of a leather womb was born again Taliessen.*
> *I can see the future and what it holds*
> *And my knowledge is as vast as the world itself."*

King Ranof was a large red-faced man with a bushy gray beard and an irritable disposition.

"Don't come before me and spout riddles and nonsense, boy! Tell me who you are and be quick about it," the king said.

So Taliessen told the king the story of how he was rescued from the weir by Gavin and raised as his son in the little cottage by the river.

"Oh ho!" said King Ranof. "Not a drop of my blood runs in your veins and yet you seek the favor of the court? Nothing your so-called father ever did was successful, and now his adopted whelp is so bold

as to ask for a boon from me!"

"I ask nothing of you," said Taliessen. "I only came to offer my service to the kingdom."

"Service! You impudent pup!" shouted the angry monarch. "You'll be of service in my prison picking oakum for a year for your insolence."

And the king's guards took Taliessen by the arms and led him off to the dank prison in the cellar of the castle, where he was thrown into a small, dimly lit cell. Now the boy-sorcerer could have easily changed himself into a linnet and flown away through the bars of his cell. But, gauging the king's temperament, Taliessen feared that some retribution would fall upon his father, and so instead he bided his time. Weeks went by and eventually word got back to Gavin that Taliessen had earned the displeasure of the king and was now imprisoned in the castle.

"Oh, why was I so foolish as to send my son to the king?" said the miserable man. "I should have known that my father would resent his fair looks and find some excuse to belittle him."

So the poor fisherman set off for the castle of his father, the king. Arriving at the castle, Gavin, by paying a small bribe, arranged to see his adopted son. Seeing Taliessen in such a sad state, the man wept bitterly and begged his son's forgiveness.

"Nay, father," said the lad. "You've done nothing wrong. And I will set all aright before long with your help.

"Father, go you to the king and tell him that, if I am not freed this day, the sun will cease to shine in the sky," said the boy.

Gavin looked oddly at his son but, knowing him to have had strange powers in the past, did as he was bid. The king, of course, flew into a rage when he heard what his son said and in response had Gavin thrown into the cell next to Taliessen.

The next day at noon, night fell on the kingdom. It was as if the sun had been swallowed by a terrible dragon. Terrified by the sudden darkness, horses shied and threw their riders. Dogs bayed and bit their masters. People old and young cried in terror, and the king's courtiers—who had heard what Gavin had told his father—begged the king to free the boy.

"Let the prisoners go!" commanded a very terrified King Ranof.

And so Taliessen won his freedom with his knowledge of when a total solar eclipse would occur—something that no one living in the kingdom had ever seen. As quickly as they could, the boy and his father journeyed back to the cottage by the river, where a very relieved mother and wife awaited them.

The next day, Taliessen went down to the weir, and where nets had been strung along the poles, he hung sheepskins instead.

His father, who had watched the boy's actions with increasing skepticism, thought, Mighty queer fish you'll catch that way. But he said nothing, for he had learned that Taliessen had the knowledge of many strange things.

And sure enough, in the morning, instead of silvery fish, the

sheepskins were heavy with a shiny yellow metal. The current of the river had deposited gold dust in the thick woolen skins! As a reward for the kindness they had shown Taliessen, the couple in the cottage by the river lived a contented life and they never were poor again. And the boy grew up to be a fine young man and had many wonderful adventures in the wide world; but the telling of those tales is for another day. . . .

CHAPTER V

The Battle of the Wizards of the North

*B*OOM-LACKA! BOOM-LACKA! Listen to the drum of Kyösti echoing across the frozen tundra!

Far, far away, up in the frozen north beyond the Arctic Circle, it is winter, cold and dark. Howling, hungry father moon, now skinny, now fat, rules the sky, and life-giving mother sun's fair face won't be seen again until spring is nigh. Ice holds the lakes and rivers prisoners to its power. Stars twinkle in the vastness of the sky. A deep haunting silence hangs over the snow-covered land.

But look! Across the sky, shimmering, dancing curtains of light appear! Brighter than the moon and stars—red, blue, yellow, purple, green, and orange—the dancing, weaving columns of color explode in the night. It looks as if a rainbow had been torn to pieces by a tornado and the scraps flung onto the black canvas of the sky.

In the long, long ago when crows were white and swans could sing, the wizard Kyösti came roaming over the frozen land. Wearing his warm cloak made from the white-bear-who-swims, he sat beneath a snow-covered fir tree and made a fire to cook a bit of reindeer meat for his supper. Before his iron pot even began to simmer, he heard in the distance the clattering of a sled over frozen snow.

"Who can be abroad in this season in such a desolate place?" Kyösti wondered.

Peering around a fir tree, the wizard soon had his answer: driving her sled pulled by a team of eight ferocious timber wolves, evil Heljä,

THE BOOK OF WIZARDS

daughter of the hunger moon, was heading directly toward him! Knowing his old enemy as well as he did and sure that she was up to some wickedness, Kyösti prepared to do battle. Beating his magic whale-skin drum covered with mystical runes, the shaman chanted a transforming spell in the direction of the approaching sled. No sooner had the incantation left his lips than the eight wolves pulling the sled turned into eight puny lemmings!

"Aaaaaiiiiiiiii!" cried Heljä. "What has become of my beautiful team? Who dares defy the great Heljä, daughter of the hunger moon?"

"Begone, you pock-faced, craven doer-of-evil-in-the-night," replied Kyösti. "If you tarry here, you will see that my power goes beyond mere shape-changing tricks!"

"Ah, I should have known it was you, Kyösti, you pusillanimous poor-excuse of a shaman," replied the sorceress. And with that she hurled a spell that caused the fir tree under which Kyösti was sitting to explode in a ball of flame. Clutching the protective amulet that he always wore around his neck, the wizard jumped clear of the fireball just in time.

"Starveling moon's brat," cried Kyösti, "you should know by now that your dark evil doings are no match for my white magic. Get you back to your netherworld and let light return to the earth."

The rivalry between these two powerful shamans was as old as time itself, and while the nature of their powers derived from very different sources, they were nonetheless nearly evenly matched. It was Heljä's intent to keep the world in perpetual darkness so that her father, the moon, could rule supreme. She loved things cold and life-less and was strongest in the winter months. Kyösti, on the other hand, drew his power from the sun and promoted fecundity and life. He longed for springtime, when he could begin his best work.

Then Heljä muttered a dark spell, and she began to grow higher and higher until she was taller than a spruce tree and she stood over her adversary, wielding a wicked-looking dagger that was longer than a man is tall.

"Your black art doesn't frighten me," said Kyösti And with that, he uttered his own incantation and grew as tall as the moon-witch and, swinging a huge club, knocked the knife from Heljä's hand.

Seeing that Kyösti had gotten the best of her, Heljä suddenly changed into a gigantic reindeer with a huge set of sharp antlers. The good wizard also took that animal's form, and the two enemies clashed together with a sound like a thunderclap. Up and down the frozen turf the two battled, each trying to pierce the other's throat with the sharp tines of their antlers. As they fought, their huge hooves dug up the ground beneath them and lakes were formed that exist to this day. Eventually it came to pass that after one ferocious attack, the horns of the two beasts became hopelessly locked and neither one could wrench free of the other.

Calling on the power of the night, Heljä turned herself into a

raging black tornado and, twisting and turning, uprooted huge trees and hurled them at the good sorcerer. Matching her spell with his own, Kyösti became a white blizzard that sent lightning and huge hailstones to batter the dark witch.

And so the battle raged across the black and frozen wasteland, with now one shaman seeming to have the upper hand, then the other seeming poised to be the victor. On and on they fought. The earth turned round and round and the stars wheeled through the sky and still the two sorcerers continued their deadly duel of magic. Just when it seemed that Kyösti had thrown his last thunderbolt and that the dark whirlwind would overwhelm him, a remarkable thing occurred. Far to the south, at the thin edge of the horizon, a tiny shaft of light appeared. It was the merest glint, but it was enough. The sun was returning to the north. Spring had come!

The tornado that Heljä had become suddenly began to shrink, its howling winds subsiding. Meanwhile, Kyösti became more powerful than ever: his magical snowstorm stunned the evil witch with a burst of jagged lightning, then battered her with hail the size of kettles, and finally covered her with a mountain of snow so deep it would not thaw for half a year. Thus ended the epic battle of the two shamans of the north, with light returning to the world and darkness vanquished once again.

And to this day, when the north is caught in the grip of ice and darkness and it seems that the sun will never show itself again, the people look at the shimmering, dancing colors against the black night sky and say, "See, the wizards are fighting!" And they smile, because they know that spring is on its way.

CHAPTER VI

The Tempest

On an island that lies in the region between the coast of Africa and the toe of the boot of Italy, there once lived an evil witch by the name of Sycorax. Her crimes of cruelty were many and lost now in the mists of time. So malevolent was she and ugly in her disposition that the powerful sorcerer Setebos, as punishment for some act of treachery, condemned her to live out her wretched life on the lonely island, with only a spirit called Ariel as her servant. Before the evil sorcerer left, with his black arts he put a curse on Sycorex, leaving her with child. This child, whom she named Caliban, was born, half man, half beast, and was of little joy to her but rather a constant reminder of her woeful lot.

Ariel, a benign spirit, refused to perform the wicked acts that Sycorax bade him do. For his disobedience, an evil spell was cast over him and he was imprisoned in a cloven pine tree. For such a creature of the air, this incarceration was the worst of tortures, and many was the night that his pathetic moaning and weeping could be heard in that gloomy place. It came to pass that Sycorax died, leaving her

spawn Caliban to roam the island, surviving on mussels, withered roots, and such husks of grain as he could scavenge for himself.

Prospero, the Duke of Milan, was a wise and learned scholar of the white magical arts. He was dearly beloved by his people, and he ruled them with compassion and judiciously saw to their well-being. He had a little daughter named Miranda whose mother, tragically, had died giving birth to her some three years previous. Though he was a

good ruler, he was, in truth, more interested in his books and the learning of magic than he was in the tedious details of government. The defense of borders, signing of treaties, adjudicating petty squabbles of lesser noblemen—all these he left for his younger brother, Antonio, to perform. The realm of learning that his library in Milan offered was enough for Prospero.

Antonio, in his duties acting for the Duke, had come to know Alonso, the King of Naples. Alonso was a treacherous man, and he coveted the rich lands to the north. To this end he hatched a plot with Antonio—who he knew secretly coveted the crown his brother wore. Under the pretext of attending a coronation in a neighboring land, Antonio and Alonso set sail in a large galleon with Prospero and Miranda on board. Their plan was to set the Duke and his daughter adrift on the high seas with neither food nor water. Nor would they provide any means to propel the vessel, leaving the two at the mercy of the wind and tide.

Luckily for the Duke, a faithful retainer named Gonzalo was aboard the ship and heard of the dastardly plot. And while he could not entirely thwart the plan, he could be of some aid to his lord. Accordingly, the night before the two were to be set adrift, Gonzalo cunningly hid some provisions under the floorboards of the small skiff, including a sail, some rigging, and a spar that could be fitted as a mast for the boat.

In the morning the Duke and his daughter were cast off from the galleon, and they sadly watched as the large ship disappeared over the horizon. Though Miranda was too young to comprehend, Prospero shed tears of grief for the desperate situation they were in but also tears of rage at the treachery of his brother, Antonio. Soon the Duke discovered the cache of supplies that the faithful Gonzalo had provided. After eating some bread and cheese and drinking a bit of water, Prospero rigged the mast and sail in the bow of the little boat and, calling up a magic wind, set off to the south.

It took a day and a night, but as a ruby red sun rose out of the sea on the second day, the two castaways saw a welcome sight: a small island lay before them. The Duke beached the craft and, shouldering his small daughter, set about exploring the island that was to be their home for the next twenty years. . . .

Prospero made a grudging servant of the truculent Caliban and, when he had freed the spirit Ariel, found in him a willing helper, so glad was he to be liberated from his arboreal prison. There was wood aplenty on the island, and soon a reasonably comfortable house was erected where the father and daughter lived a peaceful, relatively happy life. Aside from the attention paid by his adored Miranda, Prospero's greatest joy was to be found in the books that Gonzalo had fortuitously hidden in the skiff that night along with the other provisions.

The years passed, and Miranda grew into a beautiful young maiden. She was happy enough, for she knew no other life. She

played among the flowers to be found in the meadow and walked along the beach, gathering the pretty seashells that she found there. Her father taught her to read and schooled her in art and science, and they would often talk into the night about the world outside their island.

One day, as the Duke was napping after a meal, an odd dream came to the sorcerer: He saw the galleon that had abandoned them so long ago, and on its deck he saw his traitorous brother, Antonio,

with Alonso, the King of Naples, and the king's son, Ferdinand. With them was the faithful Gonzalo, now gray with age and care. Prospero awoke and, knowing this was a sign, summoned Ariel and told him what he wanted to do.

Accordingly, the spirit flew into the air and headed out to where the galleon was placidly sailing near the island in a calm sea. Ariel hovered unseen above the vessel, whistling an eerie melody, and suddenly a great gust of wind howled out of the north with such force that the sails of the boat were shredded in their yardarms. Next, curling, mountainous waves crashed onto the galleon's deck, their power sending crewmen sprawling the length of the ship. The galleon began to pitch and roll with such force that the rigging supporting the masts parted, sending the heavy spars crashing down onto the deck. All was chaos, and fearing for their lives, the seamen had no choice but to abandon the foundering vessel and throw themselves overboard.

Ariel had followed Prospero's instructions to the letter, and now he continued to do so. Though the sea was rough and many of the sailors could not swim, not a single man drowned that day. For though the sorcerer was angry at the ones who had misled him all those years ago, his vengeance did not extend to killing, and he had Ariel magically buoy up the seamen until they reached the shore of the island. He was especially solicitous of Ferdinand, who had been one of the first overboard, and he guided him to a safe, secluded cove, where he left him to rest on the warm sand. Before he departed, Ariel, still unseen, sang these words to the young prince:

> *"Full fathom five thy father lies,*
> *Of his bones are coral made;*
> *Those are pearls that were his eyes,*
> *Nothing of him that doth fade,*
> *But doth suffer a sea change*

Into something rich and strange.
Sea-nymphs hourly ring his bell."

These words greatly troubled Ferdinand as they confirmed his belief that his father had drowned in the great storm.

At the same time, the other sailors wandered about the enchanted island, suffering many hardships and tricks at the behest of Prospero through the agency of his faithful servant Ariel. In one instance, he led the men through a patch of thorns that cut them mercilessly and rent their clothes. When the traitorous seamen tried to escape this torment, Ariel caused them to be mired in a vile-smelling cesspit.

Another time the sprite lay before them a sumptuous meal, but just as they began to partake of the feast, a hideous harpy appeared—a creature with the wings and talons of an eagle and the face and torso of a woman. As lightning flashed and thunder shook the ground, the feast and the harpy vanished in a cloud of reeking, sulfurous smoke.

As harrowing as these enchantments and ordeals were, they paled in comparison with what Prospero was capable of. In the good sorcerer's own words, he told Ariel of his awesome powers:

"I have bedimmed
The noontide sun, called forth the mutinous winds,

And 'twixt the green sea and the azure vault

Set roaring war; to the dread rattling thunder

Have I given fire, and rifted Jove's stout oak

With his own bolt; the strong based promontory

Have I made shake, and by the roots plucked up

The pine and cedar. Graves at my command

Have waked their sleepers, ope'd and let them forth

By my so potent art."

Thus acknowledging the immense power he wielded through his arts, the wise sorcerer also realized that such power ultimately corrupts the man who uses it, and he made a solemn oath to renounce his art once he had had his revenge on his brother:

"I'll break my wand and bury it many fathoms in the ground and my books of magic I'll send to the bottom of the sea."

In another part of the island, it came to pass that Miranda and Ferdinand met and fell in love. Prospero observed this and approved the match.

As every tale must have an end, Prospero eventually revealed himself to his brother, Antonio, and the treacherous King of Naples, who trembled in fear before him, expecting some terrible retribution for their perfidy. But the wise sorcerer forgave them and

with these words commended his and the others' fates into the hands
of a higher power:

"Now my charms are all o'erthrown,

     And what strength I have's my own,

     Which is most faint. Now 'tis true,

     I must be here confined by you,

     Or sent to Naples. Let me not,

     Since I have my dukedom got,

     And pardoned the deceiver, dwell

     In this bare island by your spell,

     But release me from my bonds

     With the help of your good hands,

     Gentle breath of yours my sails

     Must fill, or else my project fails,

     Which was to please. Now I lack

     Spirits to enforce, art to enchant,

     And my ending is despair,

     Unless I be relieved by prayer. . . ."

CHAPTER VII

The Black School

Far in the frozen north is a land where great rivers of ice flow slowly down snow-covered mountains to the sea, and lakes of boiling water fill the air with a gray mist. Here a very knowledgeable and powerful wizard ran an academy for would-be sorcerers, called the Black School. Students traveled from near and far to learn the dark arts of alchemy, magic, witchcraft, and things of that nature.

The school was not in a building but belowground in a maze of dark tunnels carved from a single mountain. To get into the school, one had to climb down a steep set of stairs that led to a massive iron door inlaid with ancient runes and designs. There was no bell or door knocker. Those who knew the right words simply said them to the door, and if they were the correct ones, the door would open. If the wrong words were spoken—or spoken in the wrong way—no amount of banging or pleading would gain admittance. The door was so heavy that not even ten men could force it open.

One day three friends, Gunnar, Torbjörn, and Maati, who had traveled many weeks from a far-off land, arrived at the door of the

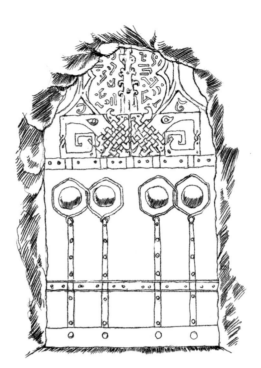

school. Each boy in turn intoned the magic words he had been taught by his village elders. They were the correct words—said in the proper way—and the great iron door, its hinges screeching loudly, opened to admit the three. Once their eyes adjusted to the gloom, they found themselves in a large cavern lit by blazing torches placed in heavy brass sconces along the walls. In the firelight they could see gleaming veins of ore that threaded through the living rock walls of the chamber. There was little in the way of furnishings beyond a few rough-hewn benches against the wall at the back of the chamber.

"Welcome to the Black School," said a low-pitched, raspy voice. "I am Wizard Steingrímur, the knower of many strange and wondrous things. Tell me why you have come to my domain."

"To learn sorcery so that I might know the future," said Gunnar.

"To become an alchemist so that I can change lead into gold," said Torbjörn.

"To gain knowledge of the sciences so that I can unlock the secrets of the earth and stars," said Maati.

"Very well," replied the Wizard, "but at the end of three years, after I have taught you what you desire, one of you must stay behind to serve me for as long as you shall live."

Now, the prospect of spending a lifetime captive in this dark world was a very bleak one. But to a young lad, three years is so far-off that it scarcely seems reachable. As it happened, so eager were they to learn the great mysteries from this Wizard, the three boys gave their assent and were enrolled at the Black School.

The very first day, the students found that the Black School was unlike any they had ever attended before. For one thing, there were no teachers; instead, there was a huge library full of magical books. A student would sit at a desk and a book would present itself, open to an appropriate page, and read itself, while the words glowed in fiery letters that seemed to be magically absorbed into his memory. Incredibly, the books never read themselves too quickly or too slowly for the pupil to grasp the subject matter. What's more, the books could tell if a student's mind had wandered or had not fully grasped a spell or incantation and would re-read the passage while the letters burned even brighter than before. Once, when Maati had stayed up late for a lesson on the astronomical arts and had fallen asleep at his desk, the book that had been reading itself closed its pages and delivered a sharp blow to the head of the sleeping boy. He never let that happen again.

The teaching methods were not the only odd thing about the Black School. The students slept on mattresses in individual alcoves carved into the mountain's walls. They needed no blankets, as a steady, soothing heat emanated from the rock itself. Meals were taken whenever a boy was hungry, and he didn't need to ask; he just had to imagine them and they appeared before him. Any sort of food at all. This was very welcome, since the boys had been away from home for some time and missed the food from their country. At their first meals the boys wished up pickled herring, gravlax, lutefisk, and dried reindeer, followed by a succession of desserts: lingonberry tarts, butter cookies, and spiced fruitcake.

In time they became more adventurous and started dreaming up exotic dishes and fruits they had only heard of or read about in books—Madras curry, Marseille bouillabaisse, and Mongolian hot pot followed by guavas, mangos, and lychees. The portions were always perfectly satisfying; never too much and never too little. And one of the best things about this magical banquet was that the dishes and silverware vanished as soon as a meal was over. No washing up!

If the boys looked forward to mealtimes a trifle too eagerly, in truth there was very little else to distract them. Study was what they were there for and study they did, morning, afternoon, and into the night. Without windows (except for a small portal high in the library's rafters for astrological observations) it was very hard to tell what time of day it was in the gloomy half-light of the torch-lit caves and tunnels. A deep booming gong that sounded the hours was the only way to know the time.

As the weeks and months unfolded, with little to distract them from their studies, the three students learned much from the strange library of Steingrímur the Wizard—the manufacture and use of amulets and talismans; potions, healing, and magical transformation; alchemy and astrology; divination and crystal gazing.

In addition to the talking books, the more practical aspects of the art of sorcery were also taught in a magical and ingenious way: by the tools themselves. Thus, when Torbjörn was learning the skill of casting alchemic spells with a wand, it was the wand that instructed him. No detail or nuance escaped the attention of the wand that was itself being wielded by the student.

"No, no! You're waving me around like you're conducting a symphony! Slower! Slower! And concentrate on the direction you're sending your spell. You'd change the whole mountain into gold instead of just that lump of lead. That's better. Try it again."

Similarly, when Maati was plotting the course of the planets and stars in pursuit of his astrological studies, the telescope and astrolabe tutored him as he observed the heavens.

"Higher . . . hold me higher. There, that's it; now sight down my arm. No! Not that one, the longer one. Now tell me what you see. . . ."

And when Gunnar was learning to see into the future, the crystal ball he was practicing on gave him this advice: "Be gentle with me. Gaze but don't stare. And don't talk so loud! Gently murmur the words you've been taught. Easy does it when it comes to foretelling the future."

In all this time, the boys had never laid eyes on Steingrímur and only a few times had they heard his deep, raspy, disembodied voice—usually when he was particularly displeased about something. If one of the boys stayed in bed a little too late of a morning, his voice, which seemed to come from everywhere and nowhere, would remind him that he was remiss. The three agreed that it gave them a creepy feeling knowing they were always being watched. . . .

So when it came to pass that the three years were drawing to a close, the students realized that unless one of them was to stay behind forever in the gloomy confines of the Black School, they had better make a plan to escape and do it soon. Though the three felt confident that they each had mastered the field of sorcery they chose to concentrate in, none was confident enough to thwart the will of Steingrímur by himself. It was agreed that if they were to succeed in making good their escape, they would have to combine forces.

Knowing that the sorcerer's dark powers extended only as far as his subterranean lair, the students knew that they would have to somehow open the door and climb the steps out of the mountain if they were to gain their freedom. But how? Ten men couldn't open the door. And even if they could, wouldn't Steingrímur appear to snatch them on the threshold? The three friends thought long and hard, and eventually a plan emerged.

First, Gunnar consulted his crystal ball to know the date when the boys' term was up—the day Steingrímur would exact his price of eternal servitude from one of them. From this they set a prior date to make their escape. Next, Maati took careful observations from his perch high in the library rafters—the reason why will be critical and reveal itself in time. When Maati's calculations were complete, the boys agreed to meet *exactly* at seven the next morning by the front door of the Black School.

That next morning as the three friends walked quickly but quietly to the school's entrance, Gunnar went first, followed by Torbjörn, holding a wand, and last Maati, wearing a loose-fitting bulky cloak. As they approached the massive iron door, Torbjörn waved his wand and, concentrating as he had been taught, murmured an incantation that turned the metal to wood! Gunnar now could easily open the door. He immediately fled up the stone stairs followed by Torbjörn, still clutching his wand.

Maati, last of the three, had just reached the first step when he felt a huge hand reach from inside the threshold and grab him by the shoulder. "You're mine!" he heard Steingrímur cry in his raspy voice. "You'll spend eternity within these walls." But Maati had known that their escape would be a close one. So, being last, he took the precaution of wearing the loose, bulky cloak—which he now slipped out of as the dark sorcerer sought to grab him. Further, by his astronomical computations, he had timed the escape to coincide exactly with the rays of the rising sun shining directly down the stairway leading to the doorway of the school.

Maati, as he shrugged out of the cloak, shouted, "I'm not the last one! Look there!" And he pointed to where he knew his shadow would be cast. Momentarily blinded by the rays of the sun shining in his eyes, Steingrímur grasped at the outline while muttering a capture spell.

Maati now joined his friends at the top of the stairway, and the

three rejoiced that their plan had worked. They were free! They breathed in the fresh air, squinting at the unaccustomed glare, and they turned their faces to the first sunlight they had felt in three years. But they made a curious sight as they walked into the East, if anyone had been on that lonely plain to see them. For though there were three of them, only two of the boys were followed by a shadow. You see, when Steingrímur fell for the ruse and cast his spell on Maati's shadow, he kept it in the Black School, and from that day on Maati never cast a shadow again.

CHAPTER VIII

The Enchantment of Merlin

Queen Morgana le Fay, the sister of the great King Arthur, was a very cunning enchantress, a mistress of magic who could weave all sorts of potent spells. She came by this lore at the court of Uther Pendragon, her father, where she was schooled by the greatest sorcerer of all: Merlin. Nevertheless, she lacked that wise man's ability to foresee the future, for it is said that no one can be taught such instinctive insight.

Morgana had come to the island of Avalon, where she brooded about the insult she felt had been visited upon her house by her brother Arthur. Such was the magnitude of her anger and resentment that, if she had been granted one wish, it would have been to see her brother dead at her feet. But Queen Morgana was well aware that she could never harm a hair on the head of Arthur as long as he was under the watchful eyes of Merlin. Merlin would be able to foresee any harm that was intended toward his king and, with his powerful arts, would prevent it from happening.

"If I am to destroy Arthur, I must first destroy Merlin," she muttered to herself.

Now, at the court of Queen Morgana there was a damsel of such marvelous and bewitching beauty as could not be found in all the four corners of the earth. Her name was Vivien, and she was the fifteen-year-old daughter of the king of Northumberland. Tall and lithesome, she was possessed of raven-black hair that set off her somewhat slanted violet eyes. It was well known that this maiden was wise and cunning beyond her years, as well as malicious and cruel to anyone who crossed her. Perhaps because of these qualities (so similar to her own) Morgana had taken Vivien as a pupil and taught her many strange and terrible things involving the dark arts, of which she knew so much. Notwithstanding all that Morgana did for her, the maiden felt not a bit of love for her mistress because Vivien was devoid of that emotion.

One evening Queen Morgana and her protégé were taking their ease in the main room of the castle, the queen on her sumptuous throne and Vivien lying on a couch covered with satin pillows. A fire was burning in a grate between them, and it cast a flickering, hypnotic aura around the sorceress and her maid.

Said the queen, "Vivien, what is the one thing you desire above all else in the world?"

"Why, I desire to possess as much knowledge and wisdom as you do, my lady," replied the maid.

This answer evidently pleased Queen Morgana, who smiled and said, "Oh, to know what I know of the world would be no great thing, but I know of a way you might surpass that goal by far and be more knowledgeable and wise than I will ever be."

"And how, pray, could I achieve that magnificent state?" asked Vivien.

As the flames in the grate slowly died to glowing embers, Queen Morgana outlined her plans for the cunning maiden. First she related the story of her own youth and how she had been taught the magical arts by the great sorcerer Merlin. She avowed that no one in the world knew more nor had more wisdom than he. And though Morgana learned well under his tutelage, she would never be as powerful as Merlin, because he did not teach her his greatest gift: the power to foresee the future. The queen said that, though the powerful wizard had many strengths and great fortitude of mind, he had one undermining weakness: he had a great love of beautiful maidens. Morgana said that the only reason Merlin had taught her as he had was because as a young girl she had been the most beautiful maiden in the kingdom.

"And you, Vivien, are even more beautiful than I was at your age," said the queen.

Then Queen Morgana proceeded to lay out a plot whereby Vivien might succeed in ensnaring the wizard in her net, using her beauty and cunning. When she had finished, the girl looked thoughtfully for a moment and then said, "But my Queen, if Merlin has the power to see the future, won't he foresee this plot to trap him?"

"Ah, but Merlin is blind to knowing his own future; he can only foresee events in the lives of others. This he told me many years ago when I was your age and held him in my thrall. To be sure, Merlin does not know his own fate," said the sorceress as shadows played on the contours of her evil face.

Before Vivien set out to do her bidding, Queen Morgana summoned a page of the court and told him to bring a certain jewel box crafted of marble and set with gemstones. She opened the box and took from it two rings: one of silver with a red stone set in it, the other a gold ring with a white stone.

"Vivien, take these two magic rings—they possess a great power of enchantment. If you wear the ring with the white stone, then the person who wears the ring with the red stone will love you with all the passion they possess and will be helpless but to do your will," said the evil queen, adding, "I think you will know what to do with them."

It came to pass that one evening, at the court of King Arthur, a grand feast was held to celebrate a great victory the king and his men had won lately on the field of battle. Many knights and lords were in attendance. Also their ladies, who were wearing their finest gowns of satin and silk and were also bedecked with all manner of precious jewels. They sat at long dining tables, partaking of the choicest delicacies

the country could provide. And there was no lack of liquid refreshment, which was evident in the din of laughter and merriment that
resounded from the rafters of the hall. During a slight lull between
courses, there entered the hall a very beautiful young damsel dressed
all in flame-colored satin, with her black hair falling like a dark
curtain over her shoulders. Her violet eyes sparkled and glistened as
if a cool light burned behind them. In her hands she carried a
marble jewel box studded with gems.

King Arthur beheld the enchanting young maiden and beckoned
her to draw near.

"Who do I have the pleasure of addressing, whose beauty is such
that it might make an angel weep?" said the king.

"I am Vivien, daughter of the king of Northumberland, Your
Majesty," she said as she bowed low before the soldier-king.

"Prithee," said King Arthur, observing the ornate box in the hands
of the maiden, "what have you in that box? Might it be a gift for me?"

"Lord," replied the damsel with a mischievous smile, "what lies
within is a ring that will fit only the wisest of men. If that be you,
then the ring is thine."

King Arthur admired the boldness of this beautiful girl but
wondered if it were not merely an attempt to flatter him to gain favor
at the court. So he was somewhat surprised when, try as he might, he
could not get the ring past the knuckle of any of his fingers.

"I guess my brawn outmatches my wisdom, eh?" said the king

with good humor. "Let's see if any of my good lords or knights might be the one the ring seeks."

With that he passed the ring to the man seated next to him, who had no more success in putting the ring on than he did. And so the silver ring with the red stone was passed from man to man until every knight and nobleman had tried in vain to wear it. With the mood in the hall so high, there was much merriment made as the ring was passed around. Finally the ring was given to Merlin, who took it and easily slid it onto his left ring finger. At this, a clamor arose and there were many good-natured remarks to the effect that the ring had, indeed, found its proper owner.

Merlin was pleased with this unexpected gift and inquired who he might thank for the piece of jewelry. Vivien was ushered into the sorcerer's presence and said, "I see that the ring has truly found its rightful owner, for surely you are the wisest of men."

Merlin looked at the maiden who had uttered those words and immediately felt a pang in his heart so excruciating that, had he not been seated, he might have fallen down from the shock. With his eyes glued to that enchantingly beautiful face, he labored for breath before he could stammer, "Whence does this ring come from, my child?"

"Sir," the maiden replied slyly, "you who are the wisest of men must have known that the ring comes from Morgana le Fay."

But because the ring was to affect Merlin's own fate, his power of

prophecy was blind to the consequences of wearing it. Moreover, the more he gazed at Vivien, the less he thought of the provenance of the ring and the more he took interest in the deliverer of the gift.

"Wise or no, even a simpleton can see that the beauty of this ring is as naught before the beauty of she who brought it hence," said the bewitched magician.

And for the rest of the feast, Merlin did not take his eyes off the sloe-eyed maiden, and she, for her part, seemed content to be the object of his attention. Others noticed the effect the girl had on the sorcerer and winked at each other, for it was widely known that Merlin had a penchant for comely young maidens.

And so the days passed and Merlin was scarcely to be seen at court. If Vivien went walking in the castle's arbor, there was Merlin walking by her side. When Vivien desired to go punting on the river, it was Merlin who wielded the pole. If hawking was Vivien's pleasure, there he was a-horseback by her side. And this continued until one day, as they sat together in the rose garden of the castle, Vivien looked Merlin in the eyes and said, "Do you love me?"

And the magician replied, "With all my heart."

"Then I want you to prove it in such a way that I will be certain that it is not merely my youth and beauty that attract you but that you admire my mind as well," replied Vivien.

"Anything I can do to prove my love and regard for you I will do it forthwith," replied the lovesick man.

"I want you to teach me all of your wisdom and knowledge of magic so that then, as equals, we might have a true meeting of the minds and I would be worthy of your love," implored the scheming maiden.

This reply had an unsettling effect on Merlin, who, though besotted by his passion for the girl, still retained some judgment and felt that all was not right with the girl's request. As he considered his answer, Vivien clandestinely rotated her ring with the white stone slowly around her finger three times.

With a sigh, Merlin finally capitulated to the base desire that possessed him and said, "Very well, my love. I will do as you ask, but it cannot be achieved here with the distractions of the court. We must journey to a place I know, and there, in solitude, I will impart to you all I know of wisdom and the magical arts."

So the two set forth the next day, on the pretext of visiting Vivien's father in the Kingdom of Northumberland. They traveled to the east on horseback for three days until they came to a dark and dismal forest with trees festooned with twisting vines that looked like intertwining serpents. While it looked impenetrable, Merlin knew the way and led them through on the winding path, deeper and deeper into the woods. So thick was the canopy of the forest that, even though it was midday when they entered it, only by using magical glowing globes could they see where they were going.

By and by, they came to the other side of the forest and, emerging, were greeted by the sight of a lush green valley with a rainbow arching over all in the springtime sun. A little way along, at the center of the vale, there was a small lake shining like a silver coin in the sun, and it was there the two travelers headed. When they reached that spot, Vivien turned to Merlin and said, "This is a very fine and beautiful place, but where will we take shelter?"

"Bide a while and you shall see," replied the wizard.

With that he closed his eyes, raised his arms, and muttered an incantation in a low, melodious voice. Even as he spoke, the earth began to tremble, and from nowhere there appeared a great whirlwind of red dust. As this whirlwind rose up into the air, many and sundry shapes could be seen within. Here a chair, there a candelabra, here a canopied bed—all appearing and disappearing in the widening gyre of the red tornado.

Then all became still and the dust slowly settled to earth, and where chaos had lately reigned, there was now a magnificent castle the likes of which has not been seen before or since.

"Oh, master!" exclaimed Vivien. "This is truly the most wondrous kind of magic that you employ! Will you teach me to do likewise so that I might build a castle out of wind and earth?" And though her words and manner were sweet and flattering, in her heart she hated the magician because she envied his power and she lusted after it with an all-consuming passion.

"This and much more," replied the sorcerer, blind to the true nature of the maiden. "But for now come into our new abode and take your ease."

And so they took up residence in the magical castle that Merlin had created, and thus began the tutelage of the wicked girl by the wise (though benighted) sorcerer. They lived in the valley for one entire year, and the sorcerer, ever in the thrall of the enchanted ring, taught the girl everything he knew in the ways of the magical arts: spells, transformations, enchantments, alchemy, and many other skills that made the sly and evil maiden a truly powerful sorceress in her own right.

When the seasons had gone through their changes and it was springtime once again, Vivien decided that there was no more to be learned from her tutor. And one day she announced that she would prepare a great feast in honor of her benefactor. Merlin, unsuspecting, was flattered at the notion and donned his finest silk robe inscribed with all the stars of the zodiac. Using the skills she had so lately learned, Vivien conjured up a dizzying array of food, both savory and sweet, and set it before the magician. Merlin eagerly partook of the food, complimenting the maiden on its variety and flavor. And the food was, indeed, wholesome and posed no threat to the hungry magician. However, the sly maid had added a surfeit of salt into certain of the dishes, and this had the result of causing a mighty thirst in her erstwhile teacher.

Acting as if it were an afterthought, Vivien produced a chalice and

said, "Sire, I have forgotten to pour you this excellent wine to accompany your feast. Please take your refreshment now and grant me your forgiveness."

Merlin, who was, in truth, quite thirsty by now, was touched by the seemingly affectionate words of the maid and was only too happy to comply. Taking the cup, he swallowed the contents in a single gulp. Immediately his mind began to cloud up in a miasma of confusion. His limbs seemed drained of their power, and he sat as if petrified, unable to move. Attempting to speak, he found himself unable to articulate the words but only uttered a low, miserable moan that, nonetheless, signified the realization of the treachery that had befallen him. Vivien, the student who had learned so well from her master, had laced his wine with a powerful potion that completely debilitated the unwary sorcerer.

Now, smiling at her bitter victory, the wicked maiden approached her former mentor and, muttering an evil incantation, stretched out her forefinger and wove an enchantment around him such that he was held as if in a gigantic silver spider's web. Merlin could not move a muscle, so powerful was the spell Vivien cast upon him. But his mind now cleared, and he could understand the words that came from the beautiful mouth of his traitorous protégé, and they resounded achingly in his ears.

"Foolish man!" said the girl, her violet eyes flashing in the night. "Did you really think that I could love you? While you lusted after

my beauty, I lusted after your power, and now I have taken it from you! No more will the world look to Merlin for his wise counsel nor to his magic for relief of their misfortunes. It is I, Vivien, who shall be the counsel of mighty kings and be adored by the masses for the power I wield."

And with those words the sorceress—for that is what she had become—conjured out of the air a coffin of stone with walls two feet thick and a monstrously heavy lid. Into this she placed Merlin, still paralyzed by the spell she had cast on him, and then set the lid securely in place. Leaving the sorcerer in his stony tomb, Vivien withdrew from

the castle and, with a flourish of her arms, caused it to disappear from sight and in its place caused a mist to rise up such that no man could penetrate it with his eyes.

So was the great sorcerer Merlin, undone by his lust for a maiden, enchanted forever by his own knowledge. His misuse of the wisdom he had been given led to his demise, and there can be no more bitter end than this: to be betrayed by another to whom you have granted power.

CHAPTER IX

Under Circe's Spell

After the long siege of Troy, Ulysses and his countrymen had been through many harrowing ordeals in their quest to return to their homes in Ithaca. With the rest of his fleet sunk by the fierce giants of Lystrygonia, Ulysses and four and forty men found themselves in their swift black boat approaching a fair and green island that was unknown to them. The men were as storm-battered as the ship, so there was great relief when they spotted a placid cove in which to find safe harbor. For two days and nights the exhausted men lay on the beach under makeshift tents—torn and frayed sails with oars serving as tent poles. Some of the men gnawed on the remaining stores from the vessel, while others scavenged the beach and hungrily devoured such clams and mussels as they could find.

On the third day Ulysses took up his bow and spear and went in search of more substantial food for his crew. Climbing up from the beach, he found a path, apparently used by game, that rose up through the thick forest that covered this part of the island. Coming

to a clearing, Ulysses could see off in the distance what appeared to be the stately towers of a palace and a tendril of smoke rising in the air. He was about to set off to investigate when his eye was caught by movement in the trees beside him. Moving stealthily, he crouched behind a nearby bush, and after first fitting an arrow into his bowstring, he waited. Presently a huge stag appeared, his flared nostrils snuffing the air as the beast slowly emerged into the clearing.

Ulysses, glad that his hiding place was downwind of the deer,

waited until his quarry was fully revealed and then carefully drew back his bowstring and let his arrow fly. The deer, mortally wounded, staggered a few feet, then, its magnificent rack of antlers swaying like branches in a wind, sank headlong to the ground. After offering thanks to the gods, the king found a length of vine with which he bound the stag's feet together. Heaving the carcass over one shoulder, using his spear as a staff, and staggering under the great weight, the mariner-turned-hunter made his way slowly back to the camp.

The men were overjoyed at the sight of Ulysses's kill, and while some hastened to build up the fire that had been smoldering on the beach, others fell to sharpening their knives to butcher the carcass. After they had roasted the venison over the flames and feasted until they could eat no more, the men lay about the camp groaning, so unaccustomed were they to such rich fare.

"This seems a good omen," said Ulysses. "Perhaps the gods see fit to show us better fortune than they have of late." He then proceeded to tell the men about the dwelling he espied while hunting. "I think we should pay a visit to the owner of that palace. But in view of all the calamities that have befallen us of late, I propose that we split up into two parties and draw lots to see which party goes exploring first." The men agreed to this, and it was done, with Ulysses heading one group and his trusted first mate, Eurylochus, the other. Putting two pebbles of equal size into a helmet, one black and one white,

Ulysses held the cup aloft and said to Eurylochus, "Pick one of these stones. If you draw the dark one, you and your party go first." Thus it was determined that, for better or worse, the first mate and his band of men would set off the next day to learn who inhabited the island.

With the dawn Eurylochus and his two and twenty men set off to see what the island had in store for them. It was not without some uneasiness that the men began their journey. With memories of the dreaded Cyclops as well as the depredations suffered at the hands of the Lystrygonians still fresh in their minds, the men were understandably nervous as they marched through field and forest to investigate the distant dwelling.

As Ulysses had indicated, when they reached the field where the deer had been slain, the men could see the tall white towers of the palace ascending out of the misty green forest that surrounded it. As they walked through the wood, every so often they would catch another glimpse of the palace, and it seemed to look more beautiful the closer they got. They soon entered a broad pathway bordered with a great variety of flowers that gave off such a sweet odor that the men felt slightly drowsy from the heady scent.

A little way along they came to a crystal-clear spring, where the band stopped to slake their thirst. Lacking any drinking vessels, the men bent over to scoop the water in their hands, but when they saw their reflections in the pool, their faces looked so distorted and odd

that they laughed out loud at the sight. The taste of the water was odd, too, though not unpleasant.

"By the beard of Bacchus," said one voyager, "I taste a bit of the grape in this spring."

Soon they came within full sight of the palace, which proved to be very large and lofty, with a number of pinnacles rising from its roof. It was now midday and the bright sun shone down on the white marble, giving it an eerie glow, as if it was illuminated from within. As they beheld this enchanting place, a light breeze from the direction of the palace bore the delicious scent of cooking meat. The band of men all inhaled the aroma deeply and with evident pleasure (as the feast of the previous day was but a memory now).

"I smell a roasting suckling pig!" cried one hungry sailor.

"It's leg of lamb with rosemary!" said another.

"No, no, you're both wrong. I smell a haunch of beef roasting on a spit!"

None of the group could agree on the precise source of the heavenly scent, but all agreed that it was heavenly. In fact, each man imagined the smell to be that of his favorite food. If the voyagers had been hesitant about approaching the palace before, their greatly heightened sense of hunger was proving to be a powerful factor in goading them on.

"It seems we're just in time for dinner," said one of the voyagers.

"Surely the owner of such a magnificent house will have some food to spare for some hungry travelers," said another.

Their previous misgivings all but forgotten, the band hastened toward the palace entrance, but before they were halfway across the wide lawn, a pack of wild beasts bounded up to meet them. Lions, wolves, jackals, tigers, and hyenas came at them in a swarm. The terrified mariners stopped in their tracks and prepared to fend off what surely was to be a vicious attack. But to their surprise, the ferocious-looking animals merely gamboled about them, wagging their tails and offering their shaggy heads to be stroked and petted, like just so many house pets greeting their master. As docile as they behaved, it seemed to Eurylochus that he perceived a menacing, if latent, evil in the eyes of the beasts. While others of the men cavorted with the strange menagerie, he kept his distance—and one hand on the hilt of his sword.

When they had gotten over their amazement, the band continued across the lawn and marched up a flight of marble steps to the large portico that gave into the palace entrance. The doors were open, and the mariners peered in at a spacious entrance hall where a fountain played in the middle of the room, its waters gushing up toward the high ceiling. The water of this fountain, by some subtle mechanism— or enchantment, would change shape as it spurted upward: now it had the shape of a man, now a wolf, then a hog wallowing in the basin as if it was a sty. But before the wanderers had time to further study this strange sight, their attention was distracted by the mellifluous sound of a woman singing in a nearby room.

"What a sweet song is that!" exclaimed one of the voyagers. "I'd like to see the face from which such lovely notes spring."

"Aye, sweet indeed," said Eurylochus, "sweet like the voice of the Sirens, who sought to lure our ship onto the rocks and us to a watery grave."

But the men could not be reasoned with. As a group they made their way toward the sound of the woman's voice. They went up to a pair of folding doors at the back of the hall and, throwing them open, passed into the next room. Eurylochus, meanwhile, hid himself behind a pillar.

Inside the room the men came upon a beautiful woman seated at a loom, where she was weaving an elaborate tapestry. At first she gave no sign of being aware of their presence but continued at her weaving, which caused the men to look at the elaborate fabric on the loom. To their astonishment, the cloth showed a lifelike picture of their recent adventures, with their own figures perfectly represented in different colored threads. Here they were with the giant Polyphemus, putting out his one, single eye. In another patch they could be seen chased by the gigantic king of the Lystragonians, who had caught one of them by the leg. Near the end of the tapestry they saw themselves on the shore of this very island, hungry and downcast, looking at the bare bones of the stag they had devoured yesterday.

Only after each mariner had examined her handiwork did the weaver turn to them in greeting. She was a tall, well-formed woman with deep-set dark eyes and a flowing mane of raven-black hair. When she spoke, it seemed that she was still singing, so sweet was the timbre of her voice.

"I bid you welcome, men of Ithaca. I am Circe, ruler of this island. As you behold, I am well apprised of the tribulations that you have faced in your journey. Believe me when I say your fate is about to change, and as evidence let me show you to the banquet room, where my servants have prepared a feast you will never forget."

The men could scarcely believe their apparent good fortune and eagerly followed the maiden to an adjoining dining hall where a long table had been set with costly silverware and golden goblets. The room was lit by huge candelabras, each holding a score of bright beeswax candles that cast a shimmering glow on the rich fabric that adorned the walls of the room. At each place was a chair so grand that it might as well be called a throne, carved of wood and gilded with gold and provided with the softest cushions made of silk, tasseled and trimmed with silver cord.

And the food! It was a veritable cornucopia the likes of which no man present had ever beheld. Great silver platters held succulent joints of meat, the head of a boar, a dozen types of fowl, jugged hare. There were bowls of all manner of soups and stews seasoned with exotic herbs and spices from faraway lands. And over a blazing fire at one end of the room, a whole side of beef was slowly turning on a spit, its juices dripping, hissing into the fire.

Attendants brought great flagons of wine from far-off countries, some of which sparkled as they were poured out and went bubbling down the gullets of the men. Other wines were a deep purple but so clear that the wrought figures at the bottom of the golden goblets could be seen as if they were naiads cavorting in a wine-dark spring. Of these and other liquors, the men took their fill, and the more they drank, the more they ate. They ate as if their lives depended on finishing every last morsel.

The men forgot the elegant surroundings they had so admired just a short time ago and descended into a gluttonous frenzy. They dropped the silver forks and grabbed whole joints of meat with their greasy hands. Spoons were discarded as the men lifted whole tureens of soup to their lips and gulped the steaming liquid directly from the vessel. In time the scene resembled a battle more than a meal, with food and drink the enemy to be vanquished! Bowls and platters clanged and clattered as they were dropped or thrown from the table. Glass flagons shattered when the wildly gesticulating mariners knocked them over, reaching for another handful of food to stuff in their craw.

If any of the band of men had had his wits about him, he would have seen a subtle change come over their hostess. Where before she had been sweetly solicitous toward them, gently urging them to partake of the bounty she provided, as the group of gourmands grew more boisterous and rude, she quietly stepped aside from the riotous scene and looked darkly at the food-stained and besotted group. Rising up to her considerable height and holding forth a thin, black wand that seemed to appear form nowhere, Circe uttered these words, and where before her voice rang out as if in song, it now raged like a terrible hurricane:

"Swine!" she cried. "You have abused a lady's hospitality. In this regal banquet hall, your behavior has been more suited to pigs in a sty. Since you have descended to the nature of pigs in every way, I shall make your appearance consistent with your true selves!"

And with those words she pointed her ebony wand at each of the men in turn while uttering a dark incantation. Then each mariner, as the wand was held in his direction, felt a queer sensation come over him. And if he looked at his hands, he could see the fingers retracting as his hand shaped itself into a cloven hoof. And if he looked at his neighbor, he would see, where there had been a familiar, human face, now a porcine visage with tiny pink eyes and floppy ears and a blunt, round snout. Lastly the men's clothing disappeared, revealing four-legged bodies covered in rough bristles. No longer suited to sitting on a chair, let alone a throne, the transformed gourmands slipped to the floor, where the clattering of their hooves resounded in the hall. Some of the men tried to groan and beg for mercy but only succeeded in filling the air with awful grunts and squeals.

Terrible to behold in her rage, Circe indicated a rear door that led to the stable yard of the palace and said, "Begone to your sty, you odious swine." And with that she aimed a few smart strokes of her wand at the departing backsides of a few of the changelings. Escaping to the yard in back of the castle, the voyagers-turned-pigs

found themselves herded into a muddy sty where offal and kitchen scraps had been tossed into a muddy trough. Incredibly, the herd plunged into this slop, grunting and snuffling as if their new form had given them new appetites as well! Eventually, when the trough was picked clean, the herd settled down in the muddy straw of the sty and fell fast asleep.

Meanwhile, Eurylochus remained where he had hidden in the entry room of the palace. For the past hours he could only vaguely hear the goings-on in the banquet room, but he had heard enough that he feared the worst for his companions. After waiting another hour to see if they would return or at least send a message, Eurylochus concluded that some great evil had befallen the men of Ithaca and hastened back to the swift black ship to give his dolorous news.

"Why do you come alone?" asked Ulysses as soon as he saw his first mate coming down the path to the camp. "Where are your two and twenty comrades?"

Eurylochus hung his head and replied, "I fear that we shall never see our comrades again." He then told Ulysses all that had happened and all that he feared had befallen his band of sailors.

The brave king lost no time, but buckled on his sword and, taking up his spear, said, "As I am your leader, it is my duty to go and see what has become of our comrades. If I can rescue them and the gods will it, I shall. Wait for me here until tomorrow. If I do not return

or send word, you must hoist sail and endeavor to reach our native land."

The remaining band of mariners were not at all pleased at these words and wished they were leaving immediately. But seeing their leader in such a fierce mood and so clearly resolved on his course of action, they could do nothing but accede to his command and heartily wish him luck in his endeavor.

Retracing his steps of the day before, Ulysses was just entering the field where he had slain the stag when he espied the god Mercury striding toward him with such a light, quick gait that he seemed to be gliding over the ground rather than walking. He wore a white tunic and had on a curious winged cap made of silver, and he carried a walking staff, also adorned with wings, around which two serpents entwined themselves.

"Hail, brave Ulysses!" said the god. "You will have need of that bravery anon. Do you not know that this island is enchanted and that Circe the sorceress lives in yonder palace? When vexed, which is often, she changes men into the form of animals that best suits their nature."

"I feared some such mischief was at play when my comrades failed to return," said the king. "Tell me, what fate has befallen my stalwart fellow Ithacans?"

"Well," replied the god, "stalwart they may be, but they are also sailors and after a long sea voyage are apt to let their appetites for food and drink get a little out of hand if the temptation presents itself." And Mercury related to Ulysses how Circe had enchanted his men and then turned them into swine.

Seeing that the doughty sea captain was greatly saddened at this news but was, nonetheless, resolved to go to the aid of his men, Mercury took pity on him (as the gods sometimes do) and, bending down, plucked a strange white flower that seemed to have grown out of the ground at that very instant. He gave it to Ulysses and then offered this advice:

"Guard this flower with your life, for it shall be your only chance to thwart Circe's evil magic. She will give you food and drink that has been mixed with potions to enchant you. Eat and drink, but before doing so, breathe in deeply the scent of this flower and it will protect you from her spells."

Thanking the god profusely for his gift and advice, Ulysses continued on his way to the palace, which loomed ever closer and more menacing with every step he took. He walked down the wide path bordered with flowers but did not tarry. Nor did he stop to drink at the spring but continued at a steady pace until he stood in front of the palace. The pack of lions, wolves, and other wild beasts slunk toward him but, brandishing his sword before him, Ulysses kept them at bay and continued right up to the portal of the palace.

Passing through the entry hall, Ulysses saw the strange fountain out of the corner of his eye. For an instant he thought that the water spout had taken the shape of a giant serpent writhing into the air, but when he looked again it had vanished. Just as his men had, the king heard the sweet singing from the next room but spent little time listening.

Throwing open the doors to the chamber, Ulysses loosened his sword in its scabbard and strode boldly into the room. Circe, who was weaving at the loom, turned to the king and said:

"Welcome, brave Ulysses. I have been expecting you. Your comrades have already partaken themselves of my hospitality, and I hope that you will accept my offer of some refreshment, too."

To this gracious offer Ulysses nodded his assent, and surreptitiously inhaling the scent of the flower given to him by Mercury, he followed the beautiful sorceress into the banquet room. This was the same place where his companions had had their fateful meal, but now, instead of a long table with two and twenty chairs, the room held in its vastness one large throne surrounded by low tables and a stool.

"Sit you here as befits your rank, Noble King," said the enchantress, indicating the comfortable seat, "and I shall serve you with my own hand so I can be certain that you get the best wine and the choicest morsels that my cellar and kitchen can provide." And with that, servants appeared bearing flagons of wine and salvers laden with all kinds of delicacies. Circe first poured a large goblet with sparkling yellow wine and said, "Slake your thirst with this, My

Lord, for I know you have come a long way in your travels."

As he raised the vessel to his lips to drink, first Ulysses took a deep draught of the flower, which he had cunningly hidden in the palm of his hand. "A very fine wine," said the king to the enchantress as he drank the cup down. "I see you don't lack for comforts on this fair island."

"I think you'll find the food of this palace is equal to the wine," purred Circe. "Let me help you to some of this choice rabbit stew." And she ladled a generous portion onto a wide silver salver.

Again, before partaking of the proffered dish, Ulysses inhaled the scent of the magical flower deeply into his lungs. "Most excellent indeed," he said as he mopped the succulent juices up with a piece of bread, "I believe I've never tasted anything better."

By now it was evident to the sorceress that the potion she had concealed in the food and drink were having no effect on the fair king. Fetching from the kitchen a quince tart that contained the ingredients of her most potent witchcraft, Circe presented it to Ulysses, saying, "I think you will find this dessert to be a truly memorable one."

Pretending to be wiping his mouth, the wily king actually took another whiff of the flower, then ate every crumb on his plate. "I agree that was truly memorable," he said with a sidelong glance at his hostess.

At this, Circe dropped the pretense of solicitousness and cried,

"Wretch! How can you eat of my magical food and stay in human form?" Pointing her black wand at the king, she continued, "I command you with all my infernal powers to take the shape of your true self. Be it a hog, go join your shipmates in the sty; if a jackal or a hyena, go howl with the beasts on the lawn. I command it!"

Rising from his chair, still in his manly form—unimpaired by the poisonous food and drink he had consumed—Ulysses leaped at the sorceress and, knocking aside her wand, held his sword at her throat. "Your power has no effect on me, as you can see. What power will stay me from cutting your cunning throat to avenge my loyal shipmates?"

Seeing that she had been bested, and finding herself not a little attracted to this powerful and clever king, Circe fell on her knees and earnestly begged for her life. "Great King, I regret my attempt to enchant you as I did your companions. If you will only spare my life, I will serve you as servant and concubine and you shall live as the ruler of this island with your shipmates restored to their former selves."

Ulysses took pity on the beautiful sorceress and, after making her swear a terrible oath to the gods that she would no longer use her powers of sorcery on him or his men, released her and bade her undo her magic. The two and twenty were restored to their former human form, and a message was sent to fetch Eurylochus and the others at the black ship by the shore. United all together, the crewmen gave a mighty cheer for their dauntless leader, and Ulysses in turn invited

them to be his guests at the palace to partake of all the joys—
untainted by dark magic—that Circe and her servants could provide.

Thus followed a year of joyous feasting—with the men remembering to show a modicum of restraint. And the voyagers were able to put from their minds the terrible events that befell them before they found the enchanted isle of Circe.

Notes

1. Baba Yaga

Baba Yaga is a traditional Russian folktale that tells the story of a young girl's dangerous encounter with a mean witch. *Baba* (originally a word used by young children) means an older or married woman or simply grandmother in most Slavic languages. She lives in a house that stands on a pair of moving chicken legs, which refer to the ordinary huts of Siberian nomadic people, who built their houses on tall tree stumps to protect themselves from bears. The stumps served as stilts to keep the nomads safe and bore a great resemblance to chicken legs. In some versions of the story, Baba Yaga is turned into an old crow at the end of the tale.

2. Coyote and the Medicine Woman

Coyotes are often portrayed as curious tricksters in Native American literature and oral traditions. In this story a wise medicine woman befriends Coyote, a constant scavenger of food. Tales such as this story present coyotes as suspicious creatures that disrupt their world but are often humiliated by their actions. However, the coyote remains cunning and faithful and represents the most basic instincts of humans and animals alike.

3. King Solomon's Ring

The power of magic is one that can be used for good or evil, depending on the wizard. King Solomon's ring is a powerful object that can make its wearer strong, invisible, free from harm, and give her/him the ability to fly. It is this ring, from medieval Jewish, Islamic, and Christian legends, that allows the man to slay the dragon terrorizing the villagers. In some versions of the story, the ring is carved with the name of God. In later versions the ring is carved with a hexagram (as in the Star of David) or a pentagram.

4. Taliessen and the Magic Potion

Taliesin was a Welsh poet in the sixth century who inspired this renowned legend from Wales. This version follows the story of a young servant boy who licks three drops of a potion of enlightenment belonging to the evil witch Bronwyn (named Cerridwin in other versions). The boy then possesses the power of inspiration and knowledge of impending events. He is reborn and renamed Taliessen (which means "radiant brow") and helps his new family to find prosperity and happiness.

5. The Battle of the Wizards of the North

The power struggle between white magic and dark art continues as the two shamans of the north battle furiously before the first signs of spring. This tale from the Baltic Sea region is a reminder that the sullen ice and darkness of the winter will soon give way to a brighter spring. The dancing colors of the northern lights (known as the aurora borealis) are often described as a manifestation of the wizards battling in the night sky. For years no one knew what caused the phenomenon, and in the northern regions these shimmering colors became the basis for many folktales.

6. The Tempest

The Tempest is a play written by William Shakespeare, considered both a comedy and a romance. Prospero (which means "good fortune") and his beautiful daughter, Miranda, are characters modeled after the Italian improvisational comedy. The half-man, half-beast character is named Caliban, a combination of the words *Caribbean* and *cannibal*. It is the magic and sorcery in the play that ties together the many characters and subplots and makes it so successful.

7. The Black School

Most Icelandic folktales feature creatures of the otherworld: trolls, elves, and other strange beings. In *The Black School*, it is the humans who are the focus in this pre–Harry Potter tale of young boys and sorcery. Many Icelandic folktales feature the devil as the ultimate villain, and *The Black School* is no different in this respect. Some versions of *The Black School* portray Sæmundur as cunningly escaping from the devil, though in this version it is Maati who escapes the devil. Such legends of strange, otherworldly creatures are common in the Icelandic folktale tradition.

8. The Enchantment of Merlin

The story of Merlin is told within the larger story of King Arthur and his knights. Merlin is a character derived from various legends and historical figures and is depicted as an old sagacious magician. Merlin is the wisest of wizards, born of a mortal woman and an incubus, an evil spirit that descends upon victims as they sleep. His powers are derived from this evil spirit, but Merlin is too wise to use them maliciously. Some of his students, however, like Vivien and Queen Morgana, use their powers against him. The story of Merlin has been reinterpreted and rewritten many times, in stories and in poems. It has even found its place on television, in movies, and in video games, too.

9. Under Circe's Spell

In Greek mythology Circe is a sorceress living on the island of Aeaea. The myth tells that Circe lives in a palace surrounded by wolves under her spell. When Odysseus and his men arrive at her palace, she serves them a feast but turns the men into pigs after seeing their ghastly behavior. The plant that saves Odysseus from enchantment is a *Moly* plant, or a white lily, common in Greek mythology. In this version of the Circe myth, the leader is referred to as Ulysses, the Latin name for Odysseus.